Pride Publishing books by Lucien Grey

Single Books
Holding onto Light

I0571281

HOLDING ONTO LIGHT

LUCIEN GREY

Holding onto Light
ISBN # 978-1-83943-968-1
©Copyright Lucien Grey 2021
Cover Art by Louisa Maggio ©Copyright April 2021
Interior text design by Claire Siemaszkiewicz
Pride Publishing

Published in 2021 by Pride Publishing, United Kingdom.

Pride Publishing is an imprint of Totally Entwined Group Limited.

HOLDING ONTO LIGHT

Prologue

Fourteen years ago

"Which one is it?"

"The golden-haired boy."

Leather-clad fingers cupped Chris' chin, yanking his head up. Chest swelling with fear, he struggled to draw enough breath.

He wouldn't cry, not in front of the other boys filling the stinking cell. He knew their sort, street-hardened thugs, ready to pounce at the smallest sign of weakness. He knew because he was the same. Though now they weren't so brave. They'd shrunk back to the darkened corners, leaving Chris dead center, their wet eyes staring at him like frightened rats avoiding the light.

He firmed his lower lip to stop it trembling, keeping his eyes tightly closed to stem the tears threatening to expose his fear.

"Open your eyes," the man holding his jaw said, so close Chris could smell the sweet apple wine on his breath.

Pressing his lips into a thin line, trying and failing to stop a sob tearing from his throat, he obeyed, blinking rapidly against the sunlight beaming in through the cell bars.

The man stared down at Chris, assessing him coolly. His face was cast in deep shadow, obscuring his features. He leaned in closer, out of the sun's glare, sniffing as he did so. Chris fought not to flinch, holding the man's gaze defiantly. His skin was bronzed by the sun, his chin and jaw heavily bristled with salt-and-pepper stubble, whereas his head was shaved, with only a hint of new growth. His dark brows were furrowed in bored assessment, deep creases forming around dark-brown eyes. He turned Chris' face this way and that. His free hand came up and stroked Chris' hair. He twisted a golden lock between his thumb and forefinger.

"He doesn't look Rasacaran."

"No, sir. A mixed blood. His mother was from the Empire, somewhere north."

How the slaver knew this, Chris couldn't fathom, for Chris had never met the woman. Though it was an easy assumption. Blond hair was a rarity in Rasacara. He didn't know anything about the northern lands of the Empire, but guessed the slaver was trying to get his money's worth by making Chris more exotic.

The man harrumphed. "A mongrel."

The slaver gave a worried look before aiming a disapproving frown at Chris, as though he were to blame for his heritage.

There was a long silence. The man's cool gaze traveled over Chris. Chris didn't like it and looked away, turning his head to escape the man's grip. It only tightened, making him whimper. Panic wracked his body. He clenched his teeth until his jaw ached. Forced to look at the man, Chris started when he noticed the man's hand move to rest on the pommel of a sword. A pistol rested on his other hip. He was a soldier. No, someone more significant, someone he should definitely fear.

"What's your name?" the man said softly.

It would be safer to give a fake name, but as Chris' gaze shifted to the man's hard eyes, he knew any lie would be as glaring as the sun bouncing off the golden pendant around the man's neck. "C-Christopher."

"Hmm. Do you mind if I call you Chris?"

Heart rattling in his ribcage, Chris said defiantly, "Only my friends call me that."

The man only laughed, a low chortle in the back of his throat, making Chris' hair stand on end. "Then that makes us friends. Here, dry your eyes. You're a man after all." He used his leather gauntlet to wipe Chris' face. Chris swallowed, ashamed he'd let his tears fall. "That's better. Now, Chris, tell me why they put you in here."

Chris' skin crawled. When he didn't answer the slaver growled, "Answer him, boy."

Chris flinched.

The soldier held up a hand to quiet the slaver. "You used magic, didn't you?"

"No," Chris gasped. "No, I didn't. I'm no witch."

The man smiled and leaned in close, his brow furrowing in sympathy. "I saw the mess you made of that city watchman. There's no possible way you could have torn an armed man apart without magic."

Chris heaved, stomach churning.

He'd been so scared. There'd been so much blood. Bones snapping under pressure. Pulp decorating the alley wall. The watchman's remains peeling from the bricks with a wet slop of crushed skin and meat. The man's lifeless eyeball staring blindly at Chris, at the filched purse still clutched to his chest, a trail of bloody gore leading back to the man's decimated eye socket.

"Want to change your answer?"

Chris stared up at the man, trembling. "He was going to hurt me. But I didn't—"

"There are witnesses. They say they saw you use magic."

Chris closed his eyes, shaking his head.

The man leaned in close and said softly, "Do you want out of this cell? If you tell me the truth, you won't be blamed for that man's death."

"I didn't kill him."

"And that's the story we'll stick to, if you agree to leave with me."

Chris opened his mouth to argue. He hadn't killed that man. He couldn't have. He wasn't capable of… Chris' stomach churned, acid bubbling up his throat. "I'm not a witch!"

The soldier sighed, clearly disappointed. He looked around the cell to the other boys. "Which ones of you want out of here?"

No one moved. The slaver frowned.

"Who saw Chris here smash that watchman into the alley wall until he crumpled into a great pile of steaming pulp?"

It took less than three seconds for the first weedy voice to pipe up. "I saw him, sir."

Chris started to tremble.

"Me too. I saw it too."

"I did too. He killed that man with magic."

"Wait a minute," the slaver tried to interrupt.

"Yeah, he squashed him flat."

"He's a witch. I saw."

Their voices grew to a roar of accusations. Chris hugged his chest, silent, angry tears falling under the deafening, condemning cries. The slaver tried to regain control, but the boys wouldn't be silenced.

He looked to the soldier. His satisfied smirk was enough to dry Chris' tears. A hot thread of energy infused the air. It was only for a second, but Chris fastened onto it and wouldn't let it go. A spark lit inside him. He pulled free of the man's grip and screamed. Fire erupted around him, a circle of flame whipping out. The boys behind him shrieked as it lashed at them. The soldier and slaver jumped back as one. Chris shot a burst of flame at the soldier. The man batted it away as though it were nothing more than a pesky wasp. Chris sagged, the strange energy he'd pulled into his body draining from him, leaving him shaky and defeated. As quickly as it had come, the light and heat dwindled then vanished.

Chris struggled to breathe. He looked down at his hands, trembling, vision blurring. *No. It wasn't me. I'm not a witch.*

If possible, the soldier's smile grew wider, losing what little warmth it had possessed. "Interesting." Turning his back on Chris, he addressed the slaver. "I'll take him off your hands. Get him prepared to receive his mark."

The slaver looked ready to argue, then stared at the black scorch marks lining the cell walls and floor. "Yes, General."

Chapter One

Present day

Sunlight injected the indigo sky with golden threads earlier each day. Spring was drawing near, its sweet scent suspended in the cold air, even as crisp frost from the persistent winter lingered, crystalizing the blades of grass into fields of sparkling emeralds.

Harry surveyed his small patch of land, watching the sun peek over the serene, silent meadows beyond the encroaching forest. It shot streaking bursts of pinks and yellows, shrinking the night sky into a mild blue, pushing back clouds as it rose, a glorious, near-blinding orange orb. Birds in nearby trees were already welcoming the dawn with their delicate song. He would never tire of waking to this peaceful serenity.

Six years. How many sunrises was that?

Shivering out the tense muscles up and down his back, Harry went to work. The cold was not a friend to the scarred muscles of his left arm, which made their complaints known as he picked up his saw. Setting his jaw, he bit the saw's teeth into the strong flesh of an oak he'd cut down and stripped yesterday.

He cut the trunk down to decent workable lengths. They would do well to replace the rotten floorboards near the fireplace, soaked with moisture from the cellar after it had flooded during the fall. It had taken weeks to dry out and create a soakaway around the house. He shouldered and lugged the timber over to the mounted flat rock he used as a dining table or a makeshift bed when the weather grew warm enough to eat and sleep outside, but right now it was his work bench. It took him most of the morning to saw the wood down to size and most of the afternoon to sand it smooth. The oak was a gorgeous color, clean and creamy for such a strong, unbending timber. It was hard-going work with only one fully serviceable arm, and it took him the rest of the day to make the new floorboards. His muscles soon began to ache, forcing him to take a frustrating number of breaks.

He'd long stripped off his coat, gloves and frayed woolen shirt, but the afternoon was already chasing away the daylight, prickling gooseflesh over his arms and chest. He sucked in his breath and shivered, basking in the cool air before pulling his abandoned shirt over his head and collecting the naked timber. A frosty night was settling in again and he didn't want the boards exposed to the elements.

He gave a lingering glance at the dying sun disappearing behind the trees, twinkling as branches swayed against their sisters.

But that wasn't all.

Something else was casting shadows in the forest, a moving silhouette that didn't belong. Harry squinted, the waning light speckling through the fluttering leaves stinging his straining eyes.

Retreating inside the cabin, Harry gingerly propped the timber against his fireside with his good arm before sprinting upstairs, taking the steps two at a time. Skidding to the floor, he pulled his rifle from under the bed. When he got back into the yard the light had dimmed to a low glimmer. Harry brought his rifle up and aimed his sights on the treeline, ignoring the tightness in his left arm and shoulder, heartbeat drumming in his temples.

All was quiet and still.

Then it wasn't.

A man emerged from a tight crop of trees and bushes, tripping over the log pile and stumbling gracelessly to the muddy ground at Harry's feet. Startled, Harry quickly recovered, gritting his teeth to steady his weak arm, his rifle trained on the man's downturned head. The man moaned and choked, picking himself up out of the mud, brushing himself down unsuccessfully, ignorant of Harry and his loaded rifle.

Harry cleared his throat. The man's head snapped up. Feral eyes glared at the barrel, then Harry. Harry's breath caught. Dying evening light reflected in the eerily familiar cobalt blue of the man's eyes.

Louis.

The stranger blinked, his lips curling into a poised smile. The illusion broke and Harry glared down at him.

"Tell me, my good man, is that your house?"

He was well-spoken, if a little effete, with a slight lilt disguising an accent. His hair, soaked from sweat and plastered to his scalp, grew past his shoulders, the color of dull gold. His wan complexion did nothing to hide the beauty of his high cheekbones and full, pale lips.

Harry grunted, remembering himself. "What business is it of yours?"

The stranger offered an uneven smile, flashing dimples in his cheeks. "Forgive me. Allow me to introduce myself —"

"I don't need your name, or any other. What is your business here?"

"I…I am merely seeking shelter, just for tonight. My carriage wheel buckled and the horses ran free of it, leaving me stranded on the road."

"The village is eleven miles south. Follow the river until you reach Paix."

The stranger gave a humorless chuckle, his smile collapsing under Harry's unwavering grimace. "It is close to nightfall. I don't wish to impose, but I'm rather desperate."

Everything about this man screamed suspicious. His clothes, though finely made, were well-worn and covered in forest debris. Mud plastered his knees and palms. Bruising blossomed under a bleeding cut on his prominent cheekbone.

Harry continued to eye him. He didn't want trouble. Yet here it was, scared and attractive and watching Harry with those painfully stunning eyes. But there was more. The way he held himself stiffly, drawing sharp breaths though he tried to hide it. He was in pain.

Harry set his jaw. He lowered the rifle. "One night."

The dimples were back, the relieved exhale quickly smothered. "Thank you so much."

"I want you gone at dawn."

"Dawn?"

"Problem?"

"No, no, dawn it is." He gestured to the house a little insistently. "Shall we?"

Already calculating over a dozen reasons not to let this man inside his home, Harry shouldered his rifle and led the way.

"Well, this is certainly…rustic," the stranger said once inside.

"You're free to try your luck in the forest."

He said under his breath, "I think I already am." He turned back to Harry, catching his scowl. "It's wonderful. Thank you, mister…" He offered his hand. It was trembling. "Surely we can be civil?" he said when Harry continued to stare in silence.

"No 'mister'. I'm Harry."

"Harry, it's a genuine pleasure." He gripped Harry's right hand. His shaking subsided a little. His palms were surprisingly rough where Harry had expected soft.

"I'm Kit."

"Kit."

"Just Kit, like you're just Harry."

Nodding, Harry released his hand.

"Don't suppose there is any food going spare?"

"Not spare, but we can share what there is."

"Wonderful."

Harry set about lighting a fire and swung the remains of yesterday's stew over the flames, the blackened pot squeaking loudly with age.

Stepping out of the cold and into the brewing heat inside the small room had brought a blush to Kit's ashen cheeks. His hands trembled at his sides. "May I?" He gestured to a chair by the fire.

Harry eyed his mud-sodden clothes. "We should get you out of your wet things."

"No." Harry flinched at Kit's vehemence. "They'll be fine. The fire will dry them soon enough." He stared into the flames, rubbing his dirtied hands together.

Harry nearly let the subject drop, but couldn't. "I don't know what you're running from, but having you die from cold in my home will bring more trouble than I need. Also, I don't want muck all over my furniture."

Kit arched his brow then glanced guiltily at the wet trail he had brought in behind him. "Of course, I apologize."

"I'll get you a blanket and something for you to wear."

"You…you're very kind."

Did Kit think him so uncivilized? Harry supposed he couldn't blame Kit after having a rifle shoved in his face. He didn't know what Kit had suffered. He didn't want to know. It wasn't his business.

With shaking fingers, Kit gingerly plucked open the buttons of his sodden coat, fine beneath the brown sludge and forest debris. He turned to Harry. Harry blinked away, heat rising under his skin.

"Would you mind giving a chap some privacy?"

Harry scowled. "Excuse me, your lordship, would you like me to wait outside?"

"No. Sorry. I just —"

Harry shook his head. "I'll go get that blanket." Begrudgingly, he left the warmth and the stranger and trotted upstairs. He tore the one decent blanket from his bed, unwilling, ridiculous as it was, to show the gentleman his moth-eaten linen stash. His clothes would be too big on Kit's lithe form, but beggars couldn't be choosers, especially beggars who arrived with nothing but the clothes on their back and suspicion circling them like flies around shit.

Harry shook his head. He'd been on his own too long to easily allow a strange gentleman into his house, into his haven.

A stranger he had left alone while his back was turned.

Swearing, he made his way quietly back downstairs, as though to catch the man in some criminal act.

Instead he caught sight of pale, naked flesh. Harry stopped in his tracks, half hidden by the stair bannister. Blood bloomed under his skin and his breath caught. It was alien for something so rare and beautiful to grace these humble, shabby walls. Kit's fair skin was marked with numerous scars consistent with sword wounds, silvery lines atop a white canvas, some thicker than others. His chest and stomach were tightly muscled, his hips tapered, swaying a little as he moved out of his trousers and bent to drape them in front of the fire. His legs were sprinkled with a light covering of hair, matching the drying locks curling into loose golden ringlets around his face.

Wetting his lips, Harry knew he should look away. Kit wanted privacy. But he couldn't bring himself to blink and risk missing a second of it. Kit's naked ass was nothing short of glorious, small and pert, muscles clenching as he shivered, gooseflesh erupting all over. Old, long-buried sensations stirred, aching inside him. Harry imagined the pebbled texture under his fingers, his tongue, bathing it with warmth until it smoothed. His lame hand clenched at his side.

Kit gingerly lifted his shirt, hissing as he peeled the fabric from his side, and Harry's unwelcome arousal withered.

Tight scar tissue stretched the skin on Kit's side just above his hipbone, a white brand in the shape of a 'W'.

Witch. An equally cruel brand, fresh and raw, outlined with inflamed flesh beside the healed scar, branded him with a distorted 'T' for tethered, a binding brand cutting off his connection to magic.

Fuck.

Kit pulled the tatty knitted throw off the chair and wrapped it tight around his body. It was too small, full of holes and dropped stitches, but it covered the brands. He clutched it to his body, rubbing his hands up and down his bare legs, wincing with every movement.

Harry breathed out a deep sigh then cleared his throat. Kit whipped around before offering a small, grateful smile. He stared in surprise when instead of offering the blanket Harry draped it around his shoulders, hoping to catch a glimpse of the wounds. Their eyes met. Heat flared and traveled from Harry's face to his chest.

Don't get involved.

He shuffled around Kit to the now boiling stew, dropping the bundle of clothes in front of the fire to warm them through. He took it off the fire and moved to a safe distance, searching through the only cupboard not holding books or tools and digging out his two least-chipped bowls. He chastised himself, but couldn't stop the urge to show this man he wasn't an unsophisticated lout. He ladled them each a hearty bowlful.

Kit muttered his thanks and hugged the bowl close before abandoning his careful manners and clamping his mouth on the lip of the bowl, gulping it down in great guttural swallows. The stew overflowed and trickled down his chin. He paused for breath only to lick the bowl clean and wipe his mouth, sucking broth from his fingers.

His eyes flicked to Harry's wide-eyed disbelief, his face growing red. "Forgive my enthusiasm. I have not eaten in days."

Harry had guessed as much. His cooking wasn't the worst, but it never warranted such gusto.

"More?" Harry offered.

"Thank you." This time Kit sipped slowly, giving a satisfying smile, dimples back in place.

They sat in silence as they ate. Kit broke it first. "I am terribly sorry to put you through this trouble."

Harry grunted. "As long as it's the only trouble you bring me."

Kit smiled weakly and lost eye contact, suddenly interested in his bowl. "I'll do my best on that score."

Harry finished his food, ruminating, fighting the urge to ask more. Bored curiosity, he told himself. He didn't need another man's problems. But his mind once more wandered back to the brands on Kit's skin, worrying about the fresh wound. He opened his mouth then quickly shut it.

Kit finished his bowl and a third before finally lounging back in his seat, sighing contently. "That was wonderful. Thank you." His smile was tired, his eyes blinking slowly.

"There's a bed upstairs."

Kit tensed. Feral eyes glinted in the firelight.

"I'll stay down here," Harry clarified calmly, as though he hadn't noticed Kit's discomfort.

Kit attempted a smile, but it looked uncomfortable on his ashen face. "That's not necessary. You don't need to give up your bed for me."

Harry gestured to his rifle. "I'll keep watch tonight."

Kit opened his mouth to argue, but Harry was not stupid and offered a skeptical brow. Someone was after this man and Harry would not be caught unawares. Kit nodded. "Thank you," he said again, his voice small. He blinked tiredly.

Harry offered Kit the clothes as he stood. Kit took them with a tight smile.

Well, better make myself comfortable, Harry thought as he watched the strange man disappear up the creaking stairs in a wobbly daze. Hooking his good arm through the back of his chair, he maneuvered it to the window. He pulled the other chair over to rest his feet on. Not the comfiest bed in the world, but he'd endured worse. He sat and watched the dark treeline, wondering what the hell he was doing allowing this man into his home.

* * * *

Kit slept despite his efforts to stay alert. He woke at the slightest noise, which was often inside this creaking shack. The entire building sounded like it could collapse under the slightest breeze. The constant throbbing soreness at his hip didn't help. Now he'd stopped running, the adrenaline no longer dampened the pain. The wound was hot and throbbing and he winced with every breath.

Growing agitated with every disruption, he rose and went to the head of the staircase. The shack was the height of simplicity, no rooms, only a downstairs and upstairs space separated by a staircase built into the wall. The bed was not the most uncomfortable he had been forced to suffer, but after years of mostly sleeping atop satin-covered, fully stuffed mattresses he'd grown soft.

The top step creaked under his light step. He hobbled gingerly down the stairs, pausing at every creak. The woodsman, kind if naïve Harry, sat at his post. Though he made a rather poor watchdog. His head was slumped on his shoulder, his bottom lip protruding a little in an endearing manner. Kit felt an unexpected urge to reach out and trace the pouting line. He had to admit the woodsman possessed a gruff, rugged charm. It was a dangerous line of thought to follow, but there was no harm in admiring the man, enjoying the rush of warmth spreading under his skin.

Looking upon Harry, armed and ready to protect his reluctant guest, Kit wondered what sort of man allowed a stranger to take refuge in his home, even when he suspected danger.

Though not friendly, Harry had offered warmth, food, a bed and protection. What would he expect in return? Kit shivered, but it had nothing to do with the cold.

Harry had an air of military about him, his body bulky, his chest and shoulders broad and his clothes, though worn and heavily patched, hugged his honed muscles deliciously. Kit leaned in close to examine the rifle dropped on his knee. It was scarred and a little beaten. The stock showed evidence of a military insignia, worn or scratched away. It was impossible to place the regiment. A percussion rifle. Definitely not a civilian weapon. Kit gave an incredulous smile, not sure if knowing made him feel better or worse.

It was not impossible for a civilian to obtain military weaponry, but Kit preferred his first and more likely assumption. Harry had been a soldier. It showed in his ability to sleep in any position, including a hard, straight-back chair near a draughty window, weapon held at the ready.

Are you a pariah too, Harry?

Kit looked into the silhouetting treeline and shivered again. He was no woodsman, a born and bred city boy, and there was no chance he'd survive out there, even if his pursuers weren't so close.

If they fell upon this hovel, would they investigate? Would Harry hand him over? Could Kit take that chance?

Kit's eyes hooded as he assessed the woodsman. He could simply kill him. Rid himself of a possible threat.

Harry's eyes snapped open. No evidence of sleep remained as he sprang up and grabbed Kit's shoulder in a crushing grip.

Kit tensed. "It's me, Kit, rememb—"

"Shush." Harry held up his hand for silence.

Kit unclenched the fist he had readied to throw in Harry's face. "What is it?"

Harry didn't answer. He crouched low at the window, bringing Kit to his knees alongside him. Kit desperately scanned the dark yard and black forest beyond, seeing nothing to trigger Harry's reaction. His grip remained on Kit while he brought his rifle up. About to ask what was happening, Kit stopped, the words caught in his throat. Scars patterned the hand gripping him. Burn marks, swirling angry scars of flames, disappearing under Harry's shirt sleeve.

A whimsical rapping sounded on the other side of the door. Kit's heart vibrated a painful rhythm in his chest. Harry didn't flinch. He motioned for Kit to stay where he was. Kit gave the barest of nods and flattened himself to the wall. Harry stood, carded his fingers through his hair, mussing it, undid the top two buttons of his shirt and gave a yawn loud enough to rival a disturbed hibernating bear. He propped the rifle beside the door frame, where it would be hidden once the door was open, but near enough at hand if occasion called for it.

Harry opened the door, one hand lazily scratching his stomach, the burned hand stuffed into his pocket. If he was shocked by who he saw, he hid his reaction well.

"Good evening, gentlemen. Can I help you?"

Chapter Two

He should have known. Harry cursed internally as he took in the two heavily armed members of the Witch Army. The Blue Crows, the very last people Harry wanted knocking on his door. Not just any Crows, but General Matthew Tariq with a second Crow at his back.

The general had grown portly in the years since Harry had last seen him and his now-white hair was shorn close to his scalp to disguise his balding spots, but it was him. He gave Harry a long, assessing look.

Harry held his breath.

This was it. This was Harry's reckoning. Strangely, he had assumed when the time came he would have resolved himself to the fact after so many years of guilt. Yet he could taste bile as fear bubbled up his throat.

Tariq spoke first. "Sorry to disturb at this late hour, but we're searching for someone. We lost sight of him in the forest, but his tracks have led us here."

The stinging bile in Harry's throat retreated. He waited, barely breathing.

There was no recognition in the general's eyes, at least none Harry could see.

Harry nodded, hoping he appeared convincingly confused and bedraggled.

"A man, going by the name Christopher Leonor, blond, blue eyes, about a head shorter than you, wearing nobleman's attire, was seen in the forest bordering your land yesterday evening. Come across anyone matching that description?"

The Blue Crows were always after someone. It was what they did. Once a mercenary band funded by the Emperor, they'd recruited witches into the Imperial Witch Army from all across the empire and beyond. But now the war was over they were nothing more than well-paid bounty hunters. They were good, efficient and brutal in their methods, and had soon found favor among nobles and gentry, covertly attacking their political or familial rivals or hunting down criminals.

Harry had to swallow before answering. "Can't say I have. Not many folk have call to come out so far, unless they're in the market for some good timber or game."

The second man, thin and angular, his mouth set in a perpetual snarl due to an unfortunate scar on his upper lip revealing buck teeth reminding Harry of a rat, gave Harry an up-and-down assessment. Harry didn't like it, but he liked even less the smile curling General Tariq's mouth.

His fingers itched for his rifle.

"It would serve as a good hiding spot. Do you mind if we have a look around your home?"

Harry's back shivered at Kit's presence somewhere behind him. There was nowhere to hide. The bed was too low to the floor to hide beneath. Escaping through the window would put him in clear view of the Crows. There was no other door than the one they currently occupied.

"Of course, sir, though I don't know how he could have gotten in."

"He's tricky. He could have snuck in while you slept."

Clenching his scarred fist, Harry had no choice but to step back and allow them access. The two men strolled in. Harry breathed slowly through his nose, steadying himself, ready to grab his rifle and take aim. He could at least take out Ratty from behind and hope Tariq's reflexes had slowed with age. The phantom smell of charred flesh momentarily gagged him. He bent low, the rifle just out of reach.

"You live out here alone, do you?"

Harry turned. The space under the window was empty except for the two vacated chairs.

Kit must have disappeared upstairs. He was still cornered.

Harry pushed the door as far as it would go, concealing the gun, ignoring the cold chill blowing in.

"Yes, sir."

"Ever go to the village Paix?"

"Sometimes, but not often." Harry's heart beat so loud in his ears he was sure Tariq must have heard it too.

"Light?" Tariq prompted when Harry just stood staring.

Harry blinked. "Of course, sir." He went around the room, lighting his small collection of lanterns and candles. He finished lighting the last then returned to the door, standing perfectly still as the Crows investigated, opening cupboards, peering around stacked timber and even looking up the chimney.

"Is the man you're searching for dangerous?"

Tariq eyed Harry for a second, the moment stretching until Harry thought he wasn't going to answer. "Nothing we can't handle. A witch."

Harry's kept his voice flat. "What's his crime?"

Tariq's brow arched. "Killed a noblewoman who was sheltering him."

Harry fell quiet as Ratty ascended the stairs, drawing his sword and pistol. Was Kit so dangerous? Whatever magic Kit possessed was useless with the tethered brand on his skin. How much of a threat was he against two heavily armed soldiers, one of whom Harry knew from experience was a powerful witch.

"You a soldier?" Tariq asked.

"No," Harry said.

Tariq squinted, regarding Harry coolly. "Could have sworn…"

Harry held his breath, Tariq's eyes boring into him.

A loud bang reverberated overhead.

Tariq copied Ratty, arming himself. Face stern, he tilted his head, listening, waiting. Harry took a step back toward his rifle. Into the agonizing silence, heavy footfalls banged down the staircase, the old floorboards protesting each step.

"Nothing, sir," Ratty reported.

Tariq deflated, giving a rueful sigh, and sheathed his sword, turning back to Harry. Harry froze in front of his rifle.

"Thank you for your cooperation," Tariq said through a tight smile. With a nod to Ratty, they departed.

Harry stood in the doorway, watching them disappear down the dirt road which led to a footpath through trees to the fields. He allowed the cold air to lick gooseflesh over his skin, reassured this hadn't been a dream. Through the gentle cries and chitters of wildlife occupying the trees and undergrowth, he heard the distinct neighing of horses and the heavy beat of their hooves being swallowed by the night.

Finally closing the door, heart vibrating in his chest, Harry flew up the stairs. His bed was on its side, blankets thrown about the floor, drawers pulled from a chest, but other than that, it was completely deserted.

"How—"

A hand caught his from behind. Before Harry could turn, his arm was twisted up behind his back. He was maneuvered around by that painful grip and shoved up against the wall, his chin colliding with a timber beam. The air rushed out of him in a startled yell. Something thin and pointed was pressed against his throat. He went rigid, scared to swallow as it pricked his skin.

"What did you tell them?" Kit breathed against his ear.

Harry snarled, "Nothing."

Kit was quiet for a moment, his grip unrelenting. "I'm sorry for this, but I can't let them find me."

"I didn't tell them anything."

Kit was silent again, his breathing harsh against Harry's ear. He hissed, "You're a witch."

Harry swallowed, grunting as metal grazed his skin. "No."

The weapon, Harry now realized, was a small, thin chisel. He could feel something else—Kit trembling. His breath came out in short, panicked bursts. "Don't lie to me. I know you have magic. That's how I found this place."

Clenching his teeth, Harry tried for calm, releasing a slow breath. "I'm not a witch. I didn't tell them anything. Let me go."

Kit growled, trembling harder against Harry's body. "No." He grunted, his pain obvious. "I can't." He gave a heaving breath as though holding back vomit. He snarled again, the trembling subsiding a little, his voice pained as he said, "I'm sorry. You might be lying. I can't take that chance."

Kit's grip shifted on the chisel.

Adrenaline spiked. Harry threw his head back, skull colliding with Kit's face. Kit grunted and staggered, the chisel grazing but not penetrating Harry's skin. Harry took the opportunity to stomp his boot down on Kit's naked foot. With an elbow to the ribs, Kit was forced back, grunting as his body took the multiple blows. Harry fingered the graze on his throat. His fingers came away clean, but he wasn't safe yet. Kit was already recovering, that feral glare back in his pale eyes, his lips curled in a silent snarl.

"Calm down."

Kit shook his head violently, squeezing his eyes shut. "Shut up."

"You need to stop. I don't want to hurt you."

Kit wasn't listening. His face was white, shining with a layer of sweat. He rushed Harry.

With a quick and precise hit to Kit's wrist, the chisel was dislodged from his grip, bouncing and rolling away as it hit the floor. Kit adapted quickly if not elegantly. Dropping low, he tried tackling Harry to the ground. Harry had just about recovered his breath when it was forced out of him again as his back slammed into the wall. Gripping Kit's shoulders, he attempted another kick only for Kit to grab his ankle, shifting his weight and dropping him to the floor.

Momentarily pinned, Harry stared up at Kit. None of Kit's haughty elegance remained, only a desperate man. His blue eyes were ablaze, teeth flashing as he put all his strength into keeping Harry down. He went for the throat, his grip strong. Harry grasped Kit's wrists, his weak left arm protesting as he struggled to pry Kit's grip apart.

The crazed blue eyes sent a jolt of hideous grief through Harry's chest. Panic and rage surged through his blood. Using his greater size and strength, Harry tore Kit's hold from his throat. Bending his leg, he wedged his foot against Kit's chest and kicked out as hard as he could, sending Kit up into the air, stumbling back and falling onto his arse. Clutching his chest, Kit fell onto his side, wheezing.

Harry coughed, regaining his own breath, rubbing his throat.

Kit's heaving didn't stop. Harry glared, controlling his anger after having a chisel aimed at his throat. Kit's eyes were enormous, his pupils blown wide. His chest expanded and contracted rapidly. Spittle wet his mouth, leaving a puddle on the floor.

Harry crawled closer, scared it might be a ruse. "Kit?"

Kit's deranged eyes met his. An unexpected tug had Harry falling forward onto his hands and knees. Something was being pulled from him, as though his very soul was being ripped from his body. Darkness lifted its head and sniffed the air.

No.

Fighting it back, he looked to Kit. His eyes were no longer stark and fearful. His pupils were rolled back into his head. Blood trickled from his nose. He gave a shuddering gasp and the pressure pulling at Harry ceased. His body felt heavy as he tried to move, exhausted as though he'd run to the village and back.

Kit's heavy dry heaves caught his attention. Harry went to him, lifting Kit's nightshirt up, modesty forgotten. Revealing Kit's torso, he was met by a red imprint of where his boot had connected with Kit's chest. Farther down his eyes were drawn to the inflamed skin around the brand. The smell of decay reached his nose. Tentatively, Harry pressed his fingers along Kit's abdomen. No broken ribs. It was amazing Kit hadn't vomited. He pressed his ear to Kit's chest. His airway didn't sound obstructed. He was having a panic attack, coupled with a high fever from the infected wound.

Opening his eyes, tears welling around them, Kit reached out. He clawed at Harry's sleeve, gasping. He looked terrified.

"Try to slow your breathing. Take deep, slow breaths or you'll hyperventilate."

Kit trembled, shakily complying, letting out a series of stunted, slow breaths. He breathed in and out, in and out, on and on until they became less haggard and a little more even.

"Good. Don't move. I'm going to examine you."

Kit flinched, but didn't move away when Harry held up his hands for calm, his face pale and eyes screwed up in pain.

With minimal prodding and some filthy, labored curses from Kit, Harry diagnosed, "Nothing's broken. But the wound on your side is infected. It needs treating or the infection will enter you blood and spread throughout your body. I'm going to put you to bed, all right?"

Harry stood and righted the bed. Kit didn't look at him as Harry gathered and cradled him against his chest and lifted him. A hissing moan escaped Kit's clenched teeth as Harry moved him, and he shivered in Harry's arms. Laying Kit down gently, Harry sighed as Kit turned away from him, gripping the edges of the blanket with shaking fingers.

"We need to draw the infection from the wound." Harry tried to turn Kit over to get at the branded skin.

Kit turned away from him. "Why are you doing this?" he asked, voice breaking, his eyes puffy and red.

Good question. Harry couldn't think of a decent answer so said, "It will hurt, but if we don't clean the infection it will kill you."

Visibly shaking, Kit grimaced as he turned, allowing Harry to see to the wound. Harry got up and went downstairs, rummaged through his medical supplies, returned with what he needed, and he set about drawing the pus from the wound. He offered Kit pain powders, which he gulped down vigorously. He cleaned the wound as best he could, working silently through Kit's occasional hissing curses and grunts of pain.

He stayed beside Kit, offering more powders until Kit fell into a fitful, exhausted rest.

Later, he left to fetch some clean dressings and a mug of water for when, or if, Kit woke. He was on guard as he returned upstairs, but he needn't have been. Kit was still asleep. His breathing was too rapid, his eyes moving under his lids as he fought off the infection heating his body.

Placing the food and drink within reach, Harry spotted the chisel still lying on the floor.

What the fuck am I doing?

Sighing, Harry returned to his post by the window, methodically checking over his gun before propping it on his knee.

* * * *

"Open your eyes, my beautiful boy."

Chris blinked slowly, his tired body quivering and sore. Last night's celebrations had run late. His master had invited all his closest friends to join in the revels.

His master had been pleased. He'd been gentle, stroking Chris' skin with reverence, leaving Chris' flittering heart thrilled. Chris had served him well.

It was strange, though, even as peace settled over Chris, as he looked into his master's dark-brown eyes, usually reassured by his all-consuming gaze, his constant hunger and possessive grip. Something was wrong.

"You did very well last night. I'm so proud of you. So beautiful." He kissed Chris' shoulder, his lips leaving Chris' skin hot, the heat almost unbearable. "So powerful. And mine." His lips moved up to press against Chris' throat, the burn growing, the heat spreading under his skin.

Chris hissed and tried to move away. He couldn't. Pain tore through him.

"What's wrong, little one?" His master's expression didn't alter, staring down at Chris.

Chris stared back. Why was he back here? Why was his master smiling at him? Was he forgiven? Chris opened his mouth, his voice cracking as he forced words out his dry throat. "You threw me away."

"Shh, my lovely boy, I would never do such a thing." He stroked a hand over Chris' cheek.

Chris cried out against the burning pain and rolled over, clutching his cheek. Eyes stinging with tears, Chris pulled his hands away. They were red. He blinked to clear his blurred vision. His hands were soaked and sticky with blood. He stared, aghast, frantically rubbing his hands together, but it wouldn't budge. The heat was growing, so was the pain.

His master's arms held him from behind. "What is all this about? Calm down. Let me hold you again. I'll never let you go, little one."

No.

Kit fought his master's grip, snarling and screaming, smearing his arms and chest with crimson streaks. His master was smiling. Kit was screaming.

Kit opened his eyes. His master was gone, but Kit could still feel him, clinging to him, staining him red.

He closed his eyes shortly after, but thankfully didn't dream, didn't remember.

When he woke again, the heat still lingered and he couldn't stop the tremors wracking his body. A face loomed over him. For a panicked moment Kit thought it was his master, but when the dark eyes caught the light they shone honey amber. Kit knew he shouldn't be reassured by the stranger's face, but couldn't fight when his heavy eyelids shut the world out.

* * * *

"How are you feeling?"

Kit was awake again, but was unwilling to open his eyes, waking for the first time without heat assaulting his body. He wanted to savor it. The pain had dulled. At some point between waking and dreaming he'd been coaxed into drinking something thick and bitter. He'd been too parched to care what it might have been and had swallowed it down willingly. Now he wanted more and it pushed him into opening his eyes, catching that amber glow once more until the woodman's face sharpened into focus.

Kit wet his lips. He coughed. Harry was at his side, holding him up and pressing a deep spoon to his mouth. As before, Kit gulped the pungent liquid down and was offered another. Giving a satisfied-sounding grunt, Harry released him gently, laying him back down on the bed. Kit winced, registering the pain at his hip.

"I'm going to check your wound and change the dressing."

Kit gave a tight nod. Harry proceeded to pull back the blanket and lift his shirt. Kit watched him remove the dressing. The wound was no longer angry, the skin around it smooth, the 'T' distorted and ugly, unfinished.

"How long was I unconscious?" His throat was full of grit.

"Three days."

Kit started. "The Crows —"

Harry held up a hand for calm. "They left and haven't been back." He cleaned the wound and wrapped new bandages around it. Kit winced and swore more than once.

"I need to go."

"No, you need more rest. You've broken the fever, but you're still healing." Harry offered him more bitter sludge.

Kit eyed him, wanting to argue, but he could barely keep his eyes open. Harry proffered the cup insistently until Kit took it and gulped it down once more with a grimace.

"I'll have some food ready for you when you next wake up. Something light."

Kit didn't sleep, fought it tooth and nail. With the Blue Crows so near, so close to finding him, he couldn't risk being caught unawares. They had to know he was still in the area, know he'd need his injuries seen to. The terrifying, chest-tightening rhythm of his heartbeat pounded in his temples, leaving him dizzy.

He was an idiot for coming here. He should have asked Harry for directions and carried on, risked running blind through the forest. At least then he would have been in better condition to fight. Now he was exhausted, barely able to move, so fucking weak his chest heaved in panicked bursts whenever he thought about how close they had come to capturing him.

His attempt to steal Harry's magic had been reckless in his weakened state. But in his panic he'd reached out desperately for anything to protect himself. Instead he'd effectively drained the last of his energy.

Why was Harry protecting him, even after Kit had attacked him? In Kit's current state he had no means to defend himself. Harry could have killed him, or thrown him out. Instead, he'd…cared for him. Laid him in his bed, brought medicine, seen to his injuries. Kit screwed his eyes shut, too pained to puzzle out Harry's motive. Too scared it would lead to questions he didn't want to answer.

Kit suspected Harry had his own reasons to avoid the Crows. He thought of the burns along Harry's arm.

Would it be enough for the Crows to overlook Kit, to distract them long enough for him to escape?

Cold sickness churned in Kit's gut. He was already scheming to betray the one man who had come to his aid. Twice. Gone above and beyond anything Kit deserved. Under his old master, he wouldn't have given a second thought about treading someone underfoot for his own gain, would have killed or sold Harry out as soon as the thought occurred to him. Things weren't as clear now.

If Harry was willing to risk himself for Kit, Kit should accept this tiny speck of good fortune with open arms.

Sometime later, after giving in and taking more powders, he opened his eyes, unsure when he had closed them, to the sound of something akin to a building collapsing. Almost vomiting up his heart, Kit bolted upright in the creaking bed, gasping at the pain radiating through his body. He made to get up, hissing when he planted his foot on the floor, the cold boards adding another deep slice of discomfort, his vision swaying after so long laying horizontal. The powders had taken away the sharp edge of agony, but he struggled to swallow back the vomit crawling up his throat, pain lancing up his left-hand side.

He spied a small window and hobbled over to it. Squinting, he blinked against the predawn light. Everything was cast in pinkish glow, the sky clear but for a few wispy clouds. The yard was half covered in shadow of the encroaching forest, but Kit could still make out Harry, on his knees, lifting and restacking a pile of rough planks — the cause of the unholy racket.

Kit swallowed. The man was a marvel. After restless nights spent guarding and tending to his troublesome guest here he was, up and working before first light, lifting heavy timbers like they weighed nothing.

Kit's breath caught watching the heavily built man, unable to help admiring the line of muscles bulging beneath his shirt. It was an enthralling sight and a bizarre comparison to the soft, compassionate man who had tended so gently to him, but then Kit remembered the boot to his chest and grimaced.

Harry favored his right arm over his scarred one. Kit grew curious. What had he suffered? What was his connection to the Crows? Why was he here, so far from civilization, surviving, Kit supposed, off the land though he obviously had medical knowledge and magic powerful enough for Kit to locate him in a forest?

Knowing any of the answers would not help either of them. Once his body recovered, he'd go and leave Harry to his peaceful isolation.

And keep running. Though he didn't know how long he could keep going before the Crows caught up to him again. He tentatively pressed a hand to the dressing on his hip. It had been a close call.

Outside Harry had downed his tools and was making for the house. Kit gingerly hobbled back to the bed. He managed to catch his breath before Harry trotted up the stairs with more food. Harry proffered the bowl and sat. They ate in silence. Kit broke it, too curious not to ask, "Why didn't you tell the Crows I was here?"

Harry flicked his gaze to Kit then back to his bowl. "I know what those bastards are capable of. I have no right to judge you."

Kit almost laughed. Was it really so simple?

He couldn't help saying, "I didn't kill her."

Harry froze, met his eyes briefly then looked away. "Who?"

"The noblewoman. I didn't kill her." He didn't know why he had to clarify this, to say it out loud, but he couldn't stop. "I worked for her as a guard, but when the Crows came asking after me she betrayed me. A fight broke out. She was caught in the crossfire."

He'd liked Lady Bordeaux, an elderly widow who'd enjoyed having a handsome man on her arm. She'd been kind and generous, which was why it had hurt so much when she'd sent the Crows after him. But he shouldn't have been surprised.

Harry stared, his gaze assessing. He nodded and that was it. He didn't say if he believed Kit or not, but Kit was glad he'd told his side.

Once they'd finished their food, Harry checked him over with a clinical eye before giving an approving grunt. Kit didn't know what he'd done to deserve such careful attention, but looking up at Harry's focused gaze, his chest swelled with gratitude and he couldn't contain it. He placed a hand over Harry's where it traced the dressing around the brand. Harry met his eyes and said, "Am I hurting you?"

"No," Kit said, his throat tightening. "Thank you. I don't know how I can repay you for this."

A strange sadness passed over Harry's face, but he dropped his gaze and said, "Rest. The quicker you heal the quicker you can leave."

It stung. It shouldn't have, but it did. Kit opened his mouth, but Harry stomped away and down the stairs before he could get a word out, bruising his sensitive ego a little more. Kit lay, listening as Harry got back to work. Eventually he fell asleep to the mechanical *thwacking* of metal on wood.

Chapter Three

Harry abandoned his work early, tired, hungry and too agitated to focus. Building, creating and fixing things with his hands usually calmed him, but right now he was too distracted.

He went inside and prepared some more stew and went upstairs. Kit lay very still, his chest rising and falling slowly. As Harry approached, Kit's eyes fluttered and he breathed in deeply. "Food?"

"Here." Harry sat cross-legged by the bed and offered the bowl.

Kit gave a small sleepy smile. It was so wretchedly genuine and vulnerable, it left Harry a little stunned and weary. Was this really the same man who had attacked him with such fear-fueled violence?

As soon as the bowl was in Kit's hands, he drank it down with as much gusto as he had that first night. Harry asked Kit's permission before touching him. He checked over his injuries. Kit's eyes were on him as he changed the bandages. Harry felt his stare.

"To say you live alone, you're well versed in caring for someone."

Harry hesitated before shrugging and answering, "I used to be a doctor."

"Used to be?"

When Harry didn't elaborate, Kit guessed, "You were an army doctor."

Harry grunted. The wound was clean. It would scar, but due to the infection would likely remain misshapen. Possibly a blessing. "What happened to not getting personal?"

"You've seen me in the altogether. I think we've crossed the line into personal territory." The haughtiness was back in Kit's voice, his accent thick again. Harry looked up and regretted it. Kit locked gazes with him, his blue eyes easily distracting and captivating.

Like Louis'.

Harry swallowed and turned away, gathering the soiled bandages.

"Why would you stick your neck out to protect the man who held a blade to your throat?" Kit asked, his brows furrowed.

Unable to hold his gaze, Harry struggled to match the two sides of Kit he'd witnessed, the desperate man ready to kill to save himself and the calm, well-mannered, if sickly, gentleman sitting in front of him. Perhaps it was a game Kit was playing, to gain Harry's trust now they were trapped together until Kit recovered. He was still pale, his eyes a little dull.

"You were hurt," he answered with a shrug.

"That's it?"

"That's it."

"I could have killed you."

"But you didn't."

Kit regarded him. "Why did you lie about being a witch?"

"I'm not a witch."

Kit laughed. "Come off it, I can almost smell the power coming off of you. It's strange, different to anything I've ever felt." Kit's eyes caught his.

Harry froze, heart pounding.

Some invisible wire wrenched at the depths of Harry's being. He jolted. A chill erupted from his chest and spread under his skin, caught and dragged to the surface. A familiar dark shadow fell over his heart, squirming to get up his throat, out his pores. He clenched his jaw, swallowing back bile as power banged and raged against its cage.

Screaming filled his ears. Men dying all around him, falling to their knees in agony, their minds broken, sinking into the bloodied earth, disappearing into a mountain of gore, swallowed up by the twisted corpses of their fellow soldiers. The terrified cries grew louder. Harry clamped his hands over his ears, but the haunting screams reverberated inside his skull.

"Harry?" Kit's shaky voice was far away.

The pull on the darkness loosened its hold and retreated. Mercifully, the terror-bloated screams of the long-dead faded. Opening his eyes, he glared at Kit. "What the fuck was that? What did you do to me?"

Kit shrank away from him. He visibly swallowed. "I... I'm sorry. I didn't —"

"Don't..." Harry gagged, shudders rolling through his body. "Don't ever do that again. You've got no fucking idea..." Harry's voice gave out. Rage and fear bound Harry's chest and mind, momentarily blinding him with images of the battlefield, red and frothing with blood.

"What was that? I've never felt anything like it." Kit's eyes were huge, almost glowing, his hands trembling.

Harry grimaced. "Something you don't touch. Promise me you won't try again."

Kit opened his mouth then wisely shut it at Harry's glare. He cleared his throat and gave a tight nod.

Harry turned from him, fear rattling his breath. There were still a few hours of daylight left. He needed to work, needed to put some distance between him and Kit. He stood, his legs a little shaky from the bolt of fear-induced adrenaline, and gathered the empty bowls.

"I'll bring some more powders for the pain later so you can sleep." He left, unable to look at Kit.

He worked, pushing his damaged limb until he broke through the pain, reaching a level of numbness that carried him through until late evening. He stopped and watched the sun disappear and the last light fade to darkness before abandoning his tools, his arms shaking, his labored breaths misting in the air. It was dropping cold, but he was numb.

This was getting too dangerous. First the Crows and now the darkness within him stirring. It was still there, resting just under the surface like a persistent wound that never fully healed.

* * * *

Three days passed. Kit had diligently complied with Harry's orders. Now he was so restless he thought he'd go mad if he didn't leave this dark little room. Harry, when he had returned, less aggravated and a little worn out, had offered him books to stave off boredom, but after ten minutes of reading about carpentry techniques and different qualities of wood, he knew as much as he'd ever want to know about both subjects and gave up. The medical texts were more interesting, but their accurate illustrations disturbed him.

By far the most entertaining distraction was Harry. Through the narrow view to the world outside, Kit admired the way Harry moved, marveling at his strength. There was no harm in looking. Harry was a man worth looking at. His powerfully built body gleamed with sweat in the sunlight, his sleeveless tunic clinging to him as it grew damp with perspiration. His bearded face was set in a serious grimace and he grunted every now and then as he labored. Little shots of arousal coursed through Kit each time he caught glimpses of Harry's gloriously tones ass as he bent low to pick up his tools or stack a pile of logs.

Kit shook his head as though it would help, recalling the touch of dark power he had pulled from Harry, unsure how to translate and understand it. Kit had experienced a wide variety of witches' magic as his master had passed him around, showing him off like a child with a new toy. Harry's was something new and strange.

He tried to focus on it, to draw it into himself, hoping Harry wouldn't notice. It had a dark, oppressive feel to it. It brought a bitter taste to his mouth. It was not the constant stream of power he had known when others used him, or when he'd begun to learn how to steal it and mold it for his own use. It was fragile and flickered like a candle. Was Harry consciously withholding his magic? Was such a thing even possible? Kit gave up, the thin, menacing tendrils leaving him cold.

He shuddered. Harry's rage when he'd prodded at the exposed vein of magic, the heavy shadow of it, the fear in Harry's eyes, had left Kit questioning his safety.

He didn't like it, didn't like not knowing what Harry was capable of, and that thought quashed the last of his arousal.

Harry visited him every day to deliver meals and to inspect his injuries. None of his former animosity showed. He was back to indifferent stoicism and grunts, which Kit found he was learning to decipher.

"Perhaps I can try standing today?" Kit said when Harry crouched over him in bed, examining his hip.

Harry gave his customary grunt, which Kit decided meant yes. Harry got to his feet and held out his hands. Kit took them and together they hoisted him off the bed. The skin around his freshly healed wound was tight. The world swayed. Kit blinked rapidly until it stopped, blotting away tears. He gingerly breathed in deeply. The swelling had gone down from his face and his chest was patterned with a colorful array of green and purple bruises. His muscles and skin throbbed like a heavy heartbeat of pain due to lack of use, but dulled as he breathed and grew used to it.

"Still hurts," Harry stated. "Can you walk on your own?"

It turned out he could, even if he moved with an ungainly wobble as he put most weight on his right leg, pulling at the scarred and healing flesh on his hip. He winced, but more out of anticipation of pain instead of the actual dull ache. The pain powders were still doing their job.

"Enough. Get back on the bed."

Harry's voice had a nice, commanding tone to it, firm, but not condescending. Kit did as he was told. He imagined Harry saying, '*Take off your clothes. Bend over. Brace yourself.*' Kit chuckled.

Harry's face shot up. "What?"

"Nothing," Kit lied. The powders must have been a stronger than he'd thought. That's what Kit blamed it on when he said, "I'll miss the attention of a handsome man once I'm healed."

He froze as soon as the words left his mouth. He was in no condition to fend off Harry if he took offense.

Harry arched an eyebrow. The left corner of his mouth curled before he dropped his gaze and lifted his hand, pointing three fingers toward the ceiling. "How many fingers?"

It was such a relief, and bizarre response to the things Kit imagined in his head, he couldn't help it and laughed again, an awkward sound, making him blush. Harry's lips twitched and he continued his examination, giving his usual satisfied grunts when Kit responded well.

"Good. Lift your shirt."

Ridiculous as it was, Kit felt a thumping wave of arousal crash from his chest to his groin. What was wrong with him? Harry had performed this same examination daily, rousing minimal attention from Kit. What had changed? He was not some virgin adolescent, sent to full mast with the slightest brush against sexual innuendo. He'd been in this bed too long, too alone. He was ashamed to admit he longed for company. Even in his early youth, he had worked the streets with a gaggle of other boys, though none of whom would have thought twice about betraying him to save themselves. Under his former master he had been surrounded by servants and would entertain a great many scores of men at his master's whim. He was not used to being alone, and had begun to grow restless in the times between meals, anticipating the comfortable silence as he and Harry ate together. Their time in each other's company was simple, unrushed and tender.

Even if Harry's touch was nothing more than clinical, Kit had started to crave those callused fingers on his skin.

Kit chewed on his lips as he lifted the second shirt Harry had lent him once it had become apparent that he was not staying only the one night. Harry ran his fingertips along the bruised skin around the brand. Kit shivered. His nipples tightened to the point of pain as gooseflesh pricked his skin. It took every ounce of his strength not to lean into Harry's touch, into his warmth.

Harry's brown eyes snapped to Kit's, a slight furrow of attentiveness on his face. "Are you cold?"

Kit swallowed. "No."

Harry went back to his examination, his dark lashes casting shadows on his cheeks. Kit's fingers itched to touch Harry's slightly curly hair, to comb his fingers through it, to pull on it until Harry looked up at him again. His fingers tightened around the blanket to stop himself.

"Sure you're not in too much pain?" Harry asked, not missing a thing.

"No." Kit released his held breath. "It feels good."

Harry's hand stopped. Just for a second. He continued. Resting his palm on the center of Kit's chest, he said, "Take a deep breath."

Kit did and Harry had him perform a few more breathing exercises, seemingly only to torment him.

Another satisfied grunt and Harry released him. He stood and moved to leave. Good. Kit could deal with the heat and perky stiffness in his trousers while Harry went about his work.

"I have something for you," Harry called back as he descended the stairs in a rush. He came back up, in his hand a rustic but sturdy-looking cane made simply with a smoothed branch. "You could do with some daylight and fresh air."

As much as the thought of leaving this stuffy room cheered him, Kit said, "You go ahead. I'll come down later."

Harry gave another grunt. "You won't make it down the stairs on your own."

Kit gave in to his dire need to see something other than the same four walls and his meager view from his small window. Harry held out a huge coat. He waited for Kit offer his arm before helping Kit into it. Harry was still being careful of him. He allowed Harry to all but carry him down the stairs, holding him close against his body, glad for the loose clothes hiding his stubborn erection. The throbbing pain on his hip soon dulled the edge of his unwarranted arousal, however.

Once on solid ground, Harry gave him the cane, releasing Kit slowly, watching him as though the second he backed off Kit would fall on his face. Offering a smile, Kit took some tentative steps to reassure Harry. He felt a bit of a pathetic fool leaning on the cane, but forgot as soon as fresh air hit his lungs and the late winter sun touched his skin.

"Try and walk around the yard a little. If you get tired you can sit over there." He gestured to a shorn tree stump.

Kit did as he was told. Harry watched closely for a time, then ignored Kit and got on with his work, sanding a length of wood.

It was nice to be moving again, but even the simplest motion was exhausting and awkward and Kit soon found his eyes wondering over to Harry. It was a much better view up close. Harry's brow furrowed as he concentrated on smoothing the grain. As the sun bathed his body, sweat gathered on his brow and trickled down his temple and jaw, soaking into his stubble. Harry didn't pause to wipe it away. Kit could almost taste it, his tongue peeking out between his lips. Dark patches began to appear under Harry's arms and down his back, making his shirt cling to his skin. Would he take it off?

But Kit was to be disappointed. Harry carried on as though Kit wasn't there. About an hour into this teasing show of rugged manliness, Kit began to grow restless again.

"Woodsman is a far cry from army doctor."

Harry stopped, but didn't look at Kit. "Yes, it is."

"Got bored of sawing off limbs but still had to put your tools to good use?"

Harry carried on. "Why do you want to know?"

Kit shrugged nonchalantly. "Just passing the time."

After a moment of nothing but the coarse grinding of sand against wood, Harry said, "I like making things. My father was a builder. He taught me. My uncle took me in later and educated me in medicine."

"Then you were drafted?"

"We both were, as surgeons."

"Not the Witch Army?"

The muscle in Harry's jaw twitched. "No."

Strange. Witches were highly valued as soldiers, more so than surgeons. When Harry didn't willingly offer an explanation, Kit asked, "Where were you stationed?"

Again, Harry paused. For a long moment Kit thought he wouldn't answer. "Rasacara."

Kit's heart jolted, blood pounding in his temples, but he covered his shock with a whistle. "Shit. How are you still in one piece?"

Harry threw down the file he'd been using and moved a little farther off to work on another piece. How did the monotony not drive him mad?

It signaled the end of Harry's willingness to talk. Kit had overstepped somehow. They remained trapped in this awkward silence until Harry finally stopped and said, "It's almost noon. I'll get us something to eat."

Kit rose to his feet quickly if not gracefully, gritting his teeth when his tight skin pulled a little. "No. Let me. I'm sure I can handle it."

Harry opened his mouth like he might argue, but instead nodded.

Kit made slow and steady progress back to the house, pleasantly warmed by unbroken sunlight, and began heating the latest batch of stew. It was rich, with a variety of root vegetables making up for the meager scrag-ends of meat Kit couldn't identify by smell, taste or texture, but it was good. Free food was always surprisingly tasty.

Trying to decide how to deliver the food to Harry without sloshing it down his front, he was saved when Harry came in, wiping his sweaty face on his shirt sleeve. "Smells good."

"Though I would love to take credit, I only swung it over the fire."

Harry gave a rare, gentle curl of his lips. Not quite a smile, but Kit would take it. Harry grunted approvingly as they both sat down to eat.

Watching Harry take a healthy swallow from his bowl, the way his throat worked and his lips kissed the rim of the bowl, Kit said, "I wish I could do more for you." Kit only noticed afterward how his voice had dropped to a husky lilt. It wasn't how he wanted it to sound, that was not what he was offering as recompense, but he was easily falling back into old habits. He needed this man's trust, and God knew that was a steep mountain to climb after his hasty stunt with the chisel. He couldn't allow himself to be left open and vulnerable. Like it or not, Harry was now his protector, but could also turn into his nearest threat. Kit needed an in, a weakness, something he could use, even as the thought set his stomach churning.

He waited, but Harry merely stared, a mild grimace darkening his features. It made Kit feel cheap. He ignored the sick twisting in his gut. It didn't matter what Harry thought of him, even though an old part of him couldn't stand Harry, or anyone else, looking upon him with repugnance. He'd grown vain under his previous master, told over and over how precious and beautiful he was, but had been cast aside all the same. The wound cut deep and still stung. A feral dog brought to heel, then spurned.

He wasn't that dog anymore, he told himself for the hundredth time. But still, he wanted this man, this lowly, isolated woodsman's attention now, his approval, when once allowing such a man to judge him would have had him baring his teeth.

Kit quickly recovered from his lapse, smiling nonchalantly, but struggled to find an opening that would loosen Harry's lips a little, reveal the smallest fragment of his soul. He had to tread carefully. Rubbing a hand through his now bristly jaw, he said, "I could do with a shave." He took a moment to admire Harry's dark furry chin. It was a little messy, but trimmed close to the skin. "Though, I don't suppose there's much access to such luxuries?"

"I'm afraid not." Harry smirked mockingly, which Kit didn't mind. Harry's smiles were charming and a little self-conscious, made even more so by their rarity. Anything was better than the perpetual scowl.

"I may sound like a pompous prick, but there's nothing wrong with wanting to look one's best from time to time, for the right reasons."

"And what would those be?"

Kit inwardly rejoiced. Harry was engaging, not shutting him down. "Oh, I don't know, depends on the company and occasion. If one needs to impress. You were in the military. Wasn't it proper for a soldier to be clean-shaven at all times?" Kit tried to imagine Harry's face without fur and found he couldn't. It suited him, adding to his rough and rugged charm.

"They were a little more lax toward the end."

It was difficult to draw a picture of Harry in his regimental wear, the black, green-trimmed, stiff cotton uniform, all prim and proper, a white and blue band on his biceps marking him as a surgeon. Did he still have it?

"How long did you serve?"

"Five years."

Odd, the minimal service required by law was fifteen years. Longer for witches. Though if Harry had been in Rasacara at the time of the Madness, perhaps he had been given early retirement. Maybe that's why he sought out quiet solitude. Hell knows what he must have suffered. Kit had heard tales. Out of nowhere, men turning and gunning down their own side, others tearing the flesh from their faces, screaming of demons, some men so strong in life, cowering and screaming until turning and eating their own guns.

Kit had spent most of the war on the Pochitarian Coast with the Navy. Witches had been pitched against heavy artillery and war machines the Rashivim Empire were sorely lacking as they relied heavily on magic. Though he hadn't seen much of the battlefield.

Harry was closing down again, his face set with a heavy grimace. So talking about the war was off limits. Fine, if it only served to hurt Harry. It was probably a time he was desperate to forget. A time Kit wished he could forget as well. The outcome of that day, when the war had ended, had taken everything he'd ever known from him.

"So, can I get away with it?" he asked, stroking the golden stubble decorating his chin and upper lip.

Harry scrutinized him, the grimace softening to another mocking smirk. "Very fetching, if a little thin."

Kit put a hand over his heart, his mouth agape in offense. "You mock me, sir. Me. Your guest and a cripple."

Harry gave a small grin again. "You're neither. If anything, you're a patient."

At least he didn't say nuisance.

"It suits you," Harry said softly. His eyes had taken on a curious warmth as he looked at the light golden hair, the same expression he wore when assessing Kit's injuries. They moved and rested on Kit's mouth, softening.

Heat spread across Kit's face. Harry blinked and said, "Are you all right? You're a little flushed."

Kit smiled to hide his embarrassment. It was one thing to flirt to fish for information. It was another to have his heart race under Harry's heated gaze. "Don't worry, it's not from sickness."

Harry was still watching him closely. Ignoring the warning in his head, Kit leaned a little closer. His breath caught when Harry raised his hand, fingertips brushing the short growth on his jaw. Kit inclined his head toward that callused touch, not realizing he'd done it until he saw Harry swallow. But he didn't move away, watching Harry's face grow conflicted and a little pained. About to ask what that expression meant, Kit stopped when Harry's palm brushed along his cheek, stroking the bristles. Growing bolder, Kit turned his head a little, his lips glancing off Harry's rough skin.

Harry's hand stopped. Kit stilled, thinking he'd gone too far, but Harry's eyes were locked on his mouth. Kit risked wetting his lips. Harry's eyes stayed fixed. He drew a little closer, his eyes glazed, his pupils huge, his mouth open the smallest sliver. Very inviting.

Harry blinked. His eyes focused. He drew back and stood, turning away from Kit. "You should keep it. The beard."

Kit wasn't letting this go. He reached out, pushing too quickly from his seat, leaving him dizzy. Taking hold of Harry's wrist, he hissed through clenched teeth as the world spun around him, "Don't go."

Harry was back at his side in an instant. He bent and reached to hold Kit steady, but Kit beat him to it, grabbing him for support. Harry met his eyes. Kit felt the fight in him building. Before he could pull away, Kit leaned in and held the back of Harry's head, stroking the thick hair under his fingers. He didn't close the gap, waiting for Harry. He had to be sure this was what Harry wanted. He thought he knew, but for a few agonizing seconds Harry did nothing except stare.

Harry's breath came in warm gusts, heating Kit's lips. He held back. Unable to stand it, Kit made it easier on both of them and closed his eyes. "I'm sorry. I thought you wanted this —"

The warm, gentle press of lips stopped Kit's words, stopped his breath, his heart. The gentleness shouldn't have been unexpected, after all the tenderness Harry had shown him. He'd known men with boyish faces who once roused rutted like mad dogs. Yet this man, with all his strength and wild appearance, was shaking when Kit kissed him back. Kit probed gently with his tongue. Harry obligingly opened his mouth, accepting and greeting it with the press of his own.

It was a wonderful surprise when Harry surged forward, quickly taking command of Kit's mouth, urging him to follow the same pace. His hands gripped Kit close. Experiencing only a hint of his strength had Kit shuddering, his cock swelling and growing heavy in his trousers.

Harry smelled glorious. His day of hard labor had covered his skin in a delightful heavy musk, the definition of masculinity. Kit wanted to taste it, to lick every inch of him clean. If he indulged in such urges, how would Harry react? What sounds would he make? But he wasn't finished with Harry's mouth yet.

There was a desperate, clumsy edge to Harry's kiss, his teeth bumping against Kit's or nipping at Kit's tongue. It felt like kissing a novice. Harry had been a soldier, a man of medicine, but his kiss was so unsure. Granted, Kit found him all the more endearing, and after so long deprived of a man's desire, felt like an inadequate teacher, but damn it if he wasn't willing to try.

Harry abruptly pulled away, shoving Kit into his seat with unexpected violence. He backed away, knocking over his chair, retreating until he hit the wall, clutching his chest and his throat, his breath coming in short, sharp wheezes.

"Harry?" Kit made to stand.

"Don't touch me!"

Magic, dark and churning, erupted from Harry. Kit readied to defend, but it wasn't targeted at him. It pumped in waves, directionless like an uncoordinated swarm, dangerous and blind, reaching out. It was raw and volatile.

Unable to run, Kit was unprepared when it touched him. It infected him, ice burning under his skin, eroding his will. He wanted to be sick, bile rising in his throat. But it wasn't bile. It was Harry's magic, tearing apart Kit's control, his body and mind submitting. He covered his mouth, tears stinging his eyes.

No. No. Can't give in to it, can't lose to it. This is my body, my mind, my will.

Chapter Four

Harry could do nothing but watch Kit struggle.

All these years fighting the darkness and he'd let his guard down so easily. It was free and he couldn't stop it.

He clawed at his skin, at his burned arm, re-carving the old scars into his skin, begging the pain to dull his magic. Blood oozed under his fingernails. He didn't feel anything.

The darkness poisoned the air, pumping its noxious venom into his haven. Panic choked him. He wanted to scream for Kit to run, knew he was too weak to even attempt it, let alone outrun the darkness. He closed his eyes, unable to watch it destroy Kit. All he could do was wait for it to be over.

He thought, as he had so many times in those early years, of his rifle, about how easy it would be to eat it. But fear, as it always had, stopped him from pulling the trigger. Peace was not meant for men like him. But now he sorely wished he had.

A harsh cough made Harry flinch. He forced his eyes open.

"Hell. You have some power there, Dr. Woodsman." Kit sat, working his jaw, stretching and shaking out his arms. "Warn a fellow next time, will you?" Kit's voice had lost its cultured edge, its lilting accent a little more prominent.

Harry found himself staring, unable to move, too fearful to even breathe in case he broke whatever strange calm Kit possessed. Massaging his throat, Kit looked to him with a worried brow and said, "You all right?"

Harry gaped before finding his voice. "Are you?"

Kit broke into a small, forced grin. "Not my first time."

Words failed Harry. He stood, wanted to go to Kit, examine and make sure for himself that this was real, that he was unharmed. But he daren't. "How?" he managed.

Kit's smile grew grim. "I... My magic..." He hesitated. "I don't possess any of my own. I am a conduit. Other witches can use me to channel their power, but I can also take it and use it as my own."

Harry had never heard of such a thing, though his magical knowledge was sorely lacking. A conduit? Was that why the darkness had stirred in Kit's presence?

At Harry's astonished silence, Kit said, "Don't worry. I've played with more dangerous bastards than you."

Harry very much doubted it, but he didn't say that. "But you controlled it. You stopped the darkness."

Kit shook his head. "No. I just stopped your will from taking control of me."

Harry deflated. He found his voice. "I wouldn't do that. I don't know how. I don't...have control." He wet his lips, unsure how much he could say without revealing too much.

"You should really work on that."

Daring to take a step closer, Harry hesitantly reached out. Blood stained the fingernails of his hand. Kit flinched out of his reach, staring at the blood.

"Are you all right?"

"I'm fine." Harry tugged his hand out of sight. "I'm sorry."

Kit snorted. "I know this is hard to believe, but I'm stronger than I look, scars and fatigue notwithstanding. That said, I think I'll go lie down for a bit."

Using his crudely fashioned cane and the bannister, Kit hobbled upstairs. As soon as he was out of sight, Harry righted his chair before falling into it. He rubbed his face in his hands. He was exhausted, inside and out, shaken to the core and close to collapsing.

Blood trickled down to his elbow. He swore and grabbed a cloth to stop the bleeding.

Kit had resisted the darkness. How? Harry wanted to go to Kit and question him, but he'd sensed Kit's unease at talking about his magic. Magic he shouldn't have access to with that brand on his side. He also couldn't be sure what questions Kit might ask in return, or if Harry could bring himself to answer them.

He'd thought it was over. He'd thought he'd buried it deep enough. But he'd never be free of it.

* * * *

"What time do you need to get back?"

60

Louis' warm breath gusting over Harry's lips, the hard press of his body crushing Harry against the coarse tree trunk had Harry scrabbling to find words to answer.

"M-my dad won't be back until sundown."

Louis leaned in and kissed him again, a smile on his lips. Harry kissed back, a little hesitant, but wanting to taste Louis, to lose himself in the heat. He closed his eyes. Louis tasted like the cherries they'd picked and eaten as they'd walked through the woods on the northern edge of the village.

"Fuck," Louis hissed, pressing closer, the hardness in his trousers grinding against Harry's, leaving him gasping and his knees trembling. "I have to be back in an hour."

"Can't you miss training today?"

Louis smiled down at him and his cheeks grew hotter. "Wish I could, but the commander will tan my hide. I'm still in trouble for missing last week's infantry drill."

If possible, Harry's face blushed further. That day was still clear in his mind. Louis had surprised and delighted him by taking Harry in his mouth. Afterward, once he'd returned home, his father had asked why he wore that stupid grin and he'd been too embarrassed to answer. "I'm sorry, soldier boy."

Louis' grin broadened as he slipped his hand into Harry's britches. Harry yelped then bit his lip. "No, you're not."

Louis was right. He wasn't sorry. He leaned in and kissed Louis again, gasping as Louis worked him in his firm grip.

"You disgusting little shit!"

Louis jumped away, spun to face Harry's father and, his face drained of all color. Utterly mortified, Harry desperately tugged his clothes back in place, his hands shaking. His father's face was purple with rage. He stepped into their little sanctuary under the overhanging willow branches, pushing Louis back with a violent shove. Louis stumbled and fell on his ass.

"Dad!"

"Don't you dare lay a hand on my son, you foul deviant," he said with his fist raised. *"Henry, come here."* He already had hold of Harry's scruff and was dragging him away.

"Dad!"

"Not another fucking word. Stay away from him. Stay away from the academy."

"But, Dad–"

"No!" He turned sharply, hand raised to strike.

Harry jumped back, eyes wide. Seeing Harry's fearful recoil, his dad wilted, pain and disappointment carved into his lined face. *"You'll go stay with your uncle Jim."*

"What? No! Please!"

"You'll do as I say! What do you think would have happened if you'd have been caught? Did you think about that? Do you think anyone will hire me if they thought my son was a..." He couldn't even put a word to what he wanted to say. *"No, you'll stay with Jim, away from that boy."*

Harry bit his lip, refusing to cry as he followed his father home, chin to his chest, teeth clamped shut, unable to look back to the willow tree.

* * * *

The earth erupted, spewing mud and blood, the explosion scattering men into pieces, fertilizing raw and beaten soil and sand with limbs and guts. Deaf to the screams of men, Harry worked to pull the living out of hell, rain crashing down around him, his boots slipping on the wet terrain, sucking him down.

"Henry, leave him," his uncle's voice called through the roaring downpour.

"But – "

"Look." Uncle Jimmy grabbed the back of his head, forcing him to look down at his patient. The lower half of the man's

body was gone, stringy, bloody remains of his intestines leaving a gory trail behind them.

The man had been alive when Harry had reached him. He'd grabbed him and tried to pull him back over their lines before another volley of bullets and cannon fire rained down on them. How had he failed to see the soldier had been blown apart?

Harry released him. Unable to dwell on the poor man's final moments, he moved to help the still-living man Jimmy was struggling to pull back to their trenches.

Upon reaching their lines, Harry and his uncle were greeted by soldiers aiding the return of the fallen into the monastery serving as their hospital. The stench of blood, piss, bile and unwashed, festering bodies engulfed the dark, enclosed space, but Harry paid it no heed once he was set to work seeing to the endless injured, dying or dead surrounding him.

As cannon fire and guns bombarded the town and surrounding land, more soldiers were rushed in. It was exhausting, with only a handful of men equipped to deal with the sheer numbers. It wasn't enough. It never was. The longer the army inhabited Rasacara the worse it became. The army was trapped with no way to enter the fortress housing what was left of the enemy's forces. They had planned to wait them out – soon they would run out of supplies and be forced out or die. That had been the plan four months ago, but the enemy endured, while their own supply ships were destroyed by storms haunting the island. Winter had set in and there was no choice but to wait it out, wait for the sea to calm and for new ships to come with either supplies or reinforcements in the spring.

Night fell and the deafening song of artillery fire finally drew to a close, to be replaced by the crazed screaming and crying of men in perpetual agony as they had their mangled limbs severed or their bleeding wounds cauterized. Some men babbled incoherently, seeing their nightmares in the waking world. Others, too stunned by the slaughter they had witnessed, were incapable of uttering a single syllable.

Harry sat staring into his rations, unable to distinguish what he was supposed to be eating. His uncle had passed him the wrapped parcel of dried meat and mashed grains to him with bloody hands. They had done what they could for the men still breathing, had even been forced to send some men back onto the battlefield with barely healed wounds.

Within the bleak, gray world his life had narrowed to inside these ancient, cold stone walls, a flash of gold sent his head snapping up and his heart pounding in his throat. He stood, his fatigue dissipating with each step he took, carefully maneuvering through the maze of men sprawled on the floor, some in cots or on bedrolls, others simply lying in any space not already occupied.

When Harry reached the blond soldier lucky enough to have a battered prayer cushion to sit on, his words came out in a rush. "Long time no see, soldier boy."

Louis jolted as though from sleep and slowly turned his head. There was a heart-rending moment before Louis' blank stare adjusted, finally seeing Harry. His blue eyes lit up as he smiled with a mouthful of dazzling white teeth. "Harry."

A little self-conscious, Harry said with a reciprocating grin, "Thought you didn't recognize me for a moment."

Though his smile never faltered, Louis said flatly, "For a moment I didn't."

Silence fell between them as Harry stared at Louis, taking in all the changes time had etched into his face.

Louis' hair had grown out a little, curling about his ears, which he'd finally grown into. His face had lost the roundness of youth and now he sported a thin golden mustache over his still very pink lips. His cheekbones stood out sharply and his chin was strong, his blond locks swept back from his broad forehead. He had surpassed the beauty *he'd possessed as a boy and had grown into a devastatingly handsome man.*

Yet even within this small slice of hell, Harry was transported back to that time they had shared while Louis had been studying in the military academy near Harry's village. He knew his cheeks must have been glowing with the memories so close to the surface.

Now here Louis was, as though no time had passed. Harry had the urge to embrace him, but fought it back.

"What are you doing here? You don't look very sick to me."

"You an expert in such matters?" There was a surprising note of bitterness in Louis' voice, which he quickly laughed off as he touched the once white now heavily stained cloth band adorning Harry's left biceps, marking him as a surgeon. The mischievous glitter in his eyes had not changed in seven years and had Harry's cock twitching with nostalgia and his heart hammering against his ribs. "So, Doctor, care to examine me?"

* * * *

Stroking the soft, glistening hair that had grown on the warm expanse of Louis' firm chest, Harry felt a comforting peace settled over him. They had come together in each other's arms as though no time or distance had separated them. The only difference was the strength and roughness of their hands. They had taken their time. The enemy had broken their constant bombardment, picking off the men being thrown at their fortified city walls, to celebrate their winter festivals in perfect safety.

Having a warm, breathing body beneath him was a novelty, the smell and taste of Louis' skin was wonderfully diverting. Louis' fingers combed through his hair. It was so comfortable, so normal and sane inside this never-ending, tedious, futile war. They had snuck inside an empty cloister, tucked themselves away with a chair wedged against the door. It was not entirely safe, but in that moment, Harry would have risked everything to keep Louis' skin pressed to his.

"Would you believe you still smell the same?" Harry said, instantly regretting letting it slip when Louis' hand stopped stroking his flank.

He lifted his head. Louis was frowning at him. He pressed his nose to Harry's temple and breathed in deeply. "Like sage and salt, but there's something new." He took another deep breath, tickling Harry's ear. "That's it," he said, pulling back with a teasing grimace. "Vinegar."

He laughed and rolled them, pinning Harry beneath him. His back was cushioned by an array of brass buttons and blood-stiffened cotton. If Louis could suffer it without complaint, so could he.

"It's in most tinctures we use."

"I didn't think you'd been bathing in it, love. Don't look so wounded."

Harry squirmed as Louis poked his side, laughing before covering his mouth with his own.

"I have missed you," Louis said as they settled down, stroking his finger along Harry's lips. "How did I survive training without our little trysts? Remember that night we nearly caught frostbite in that disused shed during my winter break?"

"It was your fault. You said the gates were kept unlocked on Wednesdays when the groundskeeper would stay out visiting the local brothel."

"I recall you pleading with me to remove my clothes. You said, 'I want to see your body'."

"You didn't refuse. You were head to toe in gooseflesh."

"It was the middle of fucking winter. But we found a way to keep warm."

"We haven't learned much in seven years."

"Oh, I don't know. You never used your tongue like that in the past."

"Never got the chance to show you."

Louis shivered. He pulled on his rumpled shirt and tucked his tunic around Harry's arms.

They didn't have much time. His uncle would be calling him back soon and after tomorrow night attempts to breach the impenetrable walls would start again in earnest, causing more death and destruction. But for now, keeping Louis close and feeling the heat of his warm body was all that concerned Harry.

* * * *

Someone was screaming. It was nothing new. Nightmares and pain gripped the men as they thrashed in their beds. But this was close and piercing. A hit to Harry's gut had him curling in on himself as more heavy blows fell across his body.

The scream was Louis'. The fists striking him were Louis'. The mad, icy, bloodshot eyes were Louis'.

Once able to draw breath, Harry gave up on defending his body and grappled for Louis' wrists, calling his name. "Louis, wake up. Louis, it's me, it's Harry."

Deaf to Harry's pleas, Louis screamed again, a terrifying wail, and tried to break free. Harry wrapped his legs around Louis' knees, pinning him in a tight hold, and rolled them. Louis' rage intensified. Harry struggled to hold him down.

"Don't kill me. Don't kill me. I don't want to die."

The terror in Louis' voice, the wide-eyed pleading stare, tore at Harry's heart.

"What's happening in there?" Loud booms against the locked door only added to the madness within. "Get this door open."

"Louis. Listen to me. You have to wake up."

Louis didn't hear him, his screams and whining pleas echoing around the chamber. Harry reluctantly released a hand and slapped Louis hard, once, twice, across the face.

There was a brief moment of clarity, his eyes finally blinking, seeing the room instead of the battlefield, seeing Harry instead of the enemy, before he fell apart, sobs racking his body. He flinched when banging at the door started up again.

Harry thought fast. He pulled on his clothes, covered Louis' lower half with his tunic and went to open the door. It was his uncle.

"What the devil are you doing in there, boy?"

"I'm with a patient." Harry swallowed the lump in his throat before diagnosing, "Mental trauma, sir."

"Him and half the men. Can't be giving special treatment to some and not others. Come on, we can't waste time on what we can't mend."

"Yes, sir." Harry glanced back to Louis. He had turned away, his back to Harry, and was shivering violently.

* * * *

"What?" Harry said. Though he had heard the words correctly, he could scarcely believe them.

"I'm going back to the front. There's nothing wrong with me and they need every able man armed and fighting."

Harry's rage and panic boiled over. "But you aren't well. Why would they do this?"

"I am perfectly capable. They're only nightmares, Harry."

"That's not true."

"Damned if it's not. Stop coddling me. I am a soldier. I need to do what I was trained for. Men are dying while I remain here taking up a bed."

"Louis, please, I've seen what trauma does to men in battle. You won't be able to fight. You'll die."

Louis forced a tight smile. "Have a little faith in me, love."

"But I can send a message, reporting you unfit, and you'll be sent home on the next supply ship."

"You can't be serious."

"Yes, all I need to do is — "

"I am not a coward. How fucking dare you."

"Louis, that's not — "

Louis took a step forward, his hand swiftly taking Harry's throat and pushing him against the stone wall. "You have no right. Just because I like fucking you, don't make me out to be some sort of pansy, hiding behind the lines, waiting for it all to be over, calling myself a doctor so I don't have to fight."

"Louis, stop," Harry choked, tears welled in his eyes, his vision darkening.

Louis blinked, and his rage diminished. "I can't do this anymore. It's over."

* * * *

"Ready, lad?" his uncle asked as they stood ready on the frontlines, waiting for the shots to cease.

"Yes, sir."

The deafening rain of bullets came to a close. "Go."

Harry set off through what was left of the streets, dodging craters in the road flooded with rainwater and bloated corpses. He saw men pinned to the floor by bullets, some so riddled with holes he bypassed them completely. For others it was still too late. He could do nothing for them. He left them to writhe and groan until they bled out.

Rain poured, hampering his vision, but he didn't slow. He came to one man, shrapnel protruding from his eye socket and the lower part of his right leg blasted away.

Harry knelt and began tying a tourniquet to the man's stump to stop the bleeding.

"Leave me."

Harry ignored him.

"Didn't you hear me? Go."

Harry didn't stop.

"Damn stubborn idiot." The soldier reached over, pulled the pistol from Harry's hip holster and pushed Harry to the ground.

"No!"

The man pressed the barrel to his temple and splattered Harry in blood, bone and gray matter.

Harry slumped in the mud, staring at the dead man, unable to breathe. Why? But he knew. No supply ships had made it to shore. Even if the man survived his wounds, there would be no returning home until this war was over.

But Harry had a job to do. He stood, amazed he was no longer trembling. Exposed and vulnerable, he hunted for more survivors.

He heard shouts up ahead.

"What are you doing, soldier? Get up and fight."

"Don't kill me. Please don't kill me."

Ice shards pierced Harry's heart. He followed the snatches of voices between blasts of cannon fire under the downpour. They brought him to a collection of rubble that had once been a building. Peering around the remains of a wall, Harry froze, his heart twisting. Louis was surrounded. Not by the enemy, who hadn't made a face-to-face appearance in weeks, but by members of his own regiment. He was cowering in filth, hands clutching the sides of his head, tears and mucus pouring down his face, his eyes crazed as he looked at his fellow soldiers as though they were strangers.

"Get up, soldier."

"Leave him. He's no use."

"Put him out of his fucking misery." The youngest of the group leveled his rifle at Louis.

Harry ran forward. Guns turned on him. He held up his hands, brandishing his white and blue armband. When no immediate shots were fired, he edged between the men and Louis, shielding him.

The young soldier kept his gun on Harry. The elder knocked it away. "Reckless fool."

Harry went to his knees, reaching out slowly to Louis, keeping his eyes on the armed men. "This man is sick. Let me take him back."

"If he can walk, hold a gun, he stays to fight," the elder man said, though Harry saw the struggle it took him to say it.

"I have to get him out of here."

"You can't help him."

Harry swallowed. He looked down at the fallen rifle that had to be Louis'. He stared at it for long moment. What would he do to save Louis? Would they gun him down before he'd even reached for it? He swallowed and turned his back on the soldiers.

"Don't kill me. Stay away." Louis pulled his pistol free.

Harry flinched. "Louis, don't."

"Stand down," a soldier ordered.

"Fuck this," another said.

"I said **stand down**."

"Louis, look at me. Don't do this." Harry held up his hands for peace.

"Soldier, I gave you an order."

"Stay away!"

A shot exploded. Harry jolted. Behind him, a body hit the ground. Smoke from Louis' pistol was swept away in the rain.

Weapons were aimed. Bullets flew.

A dark swell of blood blossomed and spread across Louis' tunic. He stared forward blindly and swayed on his knees. Harry caught him before he hit the ground.

"No, no, no, no. Louis, look at me." Harry pressed down on the wound only for another font of blood to spread across

Louis' torso. The warm spread of blood did nothing to stop cold shattering Harry from the inside.

Everything he knew, all his knowledge, and all he could do was lean over the man he loved as he bled out, his harsh, blood-gurgling breaths freezing in the air in pathetic wisps. Blood cooled and thickened in a horrendous black pattern across Louis' tunic.

Louis' wide eyes flickered, his icy glare staring but not seeing. He couldn't see Harry. There was no recognition, only fear and pain and madness. He was scared and alone in his nightmares, dying in filth and cold.

And Harry could only watch.

Louis' mouth gaped. He was trying to speak. Or scream in terror.

From somewhere in the agonizing depths of Harry's being, he found words to soothe the man he loved. "Shush, Louis, it's all right now. You don't have to fear anything anymore. They can't touch you now."

Enemy fire filled the air, shaking the earth as shells and cannon balls fell around them. Through the chaos, Harry doubted his words reached Louis.

Gritting his teeth, Harry watched his tears cascade in cold rivers over Louis' ashen face.

The death throes gripping Louis' body stopped. He fell still, the terror and his life leaving him. Before he drew his last breath, he broke Harry's heart completely with the smile he reserved only for Harry. The smallest curl to the edges of his lips, his eyes crinkled a little.

He was gone. The smile remained. He was at peace.

Harry's brittle resolve crumbled. The sound he emitted failed to express his agony. He couldn't stop the scream ripping through his chest and throat. Wails of grief gave out to an airless sob. He couldn't breathe. His chest was constricted, cold bands of spiked steel crushing it until he was forced to draw breath through his raging cries.

The cannon fire and explosions stopped. The rain of bullets subsided. More men were dead or dying. Louis was dead. Everything was over.

Harry wiped the blood from Louis' pink lips with his rain-moistened sleeve, closed his blue eyes from the unfeeling world and brushed his golden hair back into place. It was tangled from the rain.

"What are you doing? We need to advance. Get up. Leave him."

Harry pulled Louis close, leeching the last of Louis' heat and clinging to it.

"Leave them both."

"Don't be an idiot. He's a doctor."

Harry bent to kiss Louis' mouth, forgiving the last poisonous words Louis had spoken to him. Too cold – their kisses had always held so much heat.

"Fucking disgusting. We should bury a bullet in him before he infects the men."

"That's enough."

"Letting a man like that touch injured men when they can't defend themselves makes me sick to my stomach."

A rifle was primed.

A great swell of adrenaline swept through Harry with such sudden severity he fell to all fours clutching great fistfuls of soil. His heart vibrated hard and fast in his chest. His vision darkened at the edges as his breath failed to keep pace.

Shadow engulfed him, darkness so complete, so filled with malice and rage, he couldn't fight it. All his pain and his grief surged up, swallowing him.

He fought the urge to vomit. His jaw fell open. He tried to scream and retch, but nothing would come. Nonetheless, he felt relief. The pressure inside him had been punctured.

Harry turned to the soldiers. The eldest was on his knees, clutching his skull, rocking back and forth, muttering.

Another soldier was staring about at the gruesome chaos around them, desperately brushing his arms and torso as though ghosts pulled at him. He was screaming.

The battleground erupted with the horrified wails of men. Gun and cannon fire exploded all around Harry. He should have dropped to his belly, or taken cover behind the crumbling buildings but his limbs were rigid, his fists locked, his entire core thrumming with waves of overwhelming…power. There was no other word for it. Raw, aching throbs of power, erupting from his mouth, eyes, nose, skin, his every pore tearing apart to release it into the atmosphere.

Soldiers were coming. They were running, their rapid charge serving as warning until they fell upon the scene of their slaughtered comrades.

Harry's desire to flee dulled then vanished as though the armed wall of men were nothing more than a disturbed nest of spiders. Harry stood firm as they came within range. Battle rage fell from their faces. Their courageous cries sputtered out.

A great rumbling sounded. In the distance, the great stone gates of the fortress were opening. For the first time since Harry had set foot on the island the enormous impregnable walls were shifting, blowing great waves of mud and debris into the air. The enemy were preparing to engage, after all this time.

But there was no charge.

The screams that filled the air were not battle cries. They stretched from both sides of the island, ear-shattering roars of utter panic and madness.

Harry wanted to cover his ears, unable to bear it. But the power raging through and enveloping him held him fast, bringing with it a rumbling thrill filling his chest and stomach. There was elation, a disturbing joy erupting with such immense power. His body convulsed, his heart almost rupturing under the strength of it.

He closed his eyes for what seemed like seconds on the exhilarating horror. When he opened them he was surrounded on all sides. Fellow Rashivims and hundreds of the enemy deep in battle. No formation. No sides of the battlefield. Some fought without weapons, leaping and gouging out the eyes of the enemy. No, not the enemy. This soldier was attacking his comrade, his brother in arms. Another turned on his fellow soldier, tearing into his guts with a bayonet, laughing hysterically as intestines poured to the ground. He turned the rifle on himself and drove it into his throat, choking on his laughter.

The enemy showed no comprehension of who to fight, choosing the men at their sides, screaming as though staring upon demons, running or cowering on the soiled ground or driving blades and firing bullets into men wearing their own colors.

Harry stood amidst them all, blood and filth splashing his face, spurting in great gouts over his tunic. No shots hit him. Men fell at his feet, injured or dying, some fighting fiercely, almost but never touching him. They didn't even glance his way, lost in frenzied madness.

A soldier bent close, his eyes glazed with lunacy, a pike raised in his hands, ready to drive the point into Louis' chest. Another pulse of darkness radiated from Harry as he breathed in to cry rage at the solider. The man dropped the pike, screwing his eyes shut, squeezing the sides of his head, shuddering from head to toe. A bayonet erupted from his mouth. It was pulled out by a blood-soaked soldier. He proceeded to spear the man to the ground repeatedly.

Convulsions wracked Harry's body. He was the orchestrator of this horror. This power, this magic...his magic was driving these men to kill indiscriminately, to fall on their own weapons in fear and madness.

He fell to the ground, gathering Louis into his arms, closing his eyes to the bloodshed. His fingers shook with the effort to stop whatever was happening. He couldn't. He didn't know how. He couldn't gather his scattered will. He was falling apart, clutching desperately to Louis' cooling body.

Until the battlefield fell into deafening silence.

Opening his eyes, he shakily took in a blood-reddened battleground, the ruined town, butchered bodies of men wearing the colors of both armies piled high. His entire body trembled. The air was rank with death.

He had to get Louis out of there. It was the only thought that got him moving. It took all of his waning strength to drag Louis' body out of the gore, only to be hindered by the wall of corpses surrounding them. Desperately he fought through severed limbs, pulling guts from his skin, his clothes sodden with mud, blood and bile, the vile rotten stink of it sinking into his skin, drowning him.

He clung to Louis, grunting and crying as he went. Pulling Louis over the pile of men, Louis' lifeless bulk may as well have weighed a thousand tons.

"Come on, soldier boy," Harry spluttered, exhausted, tears soaked with mud and blood running into his nose and mouth. He pulled desperately at Louis' arm to get him over the mound. He felt his palm slipping. Blood weakened his hold. Louis' arm slid from his grasp, his fingernails tearing into Louis' skin. He fell into the gore, his landing softened by dead soldiers. Staring at the four red tracks he'd made in Louis' arm, seeing the cold blood trickle softly over his filthy gray skin, Harry collapsed back and screamed.

Chapter Five

Screams penetrated Kit's sleep. Stiff and aching, he hobbled down the stairs. Through the gloom he saw Harry lying on the floor, his chair toppled over from where he must have fallen. Eyes screwed shut, he thrashed on the floor, his mouth thrown open in agonized howls. A shadow of invisible power enclosed him, pulsing and spreading out into the room. Kit dropped to his knees, careful to stay out of reach. He daren't let the shroud of magic touch him. If it took hold of him, he didn't know if he was strong enough to fight it off again.

"Harry! Wake up."

Harry's eyes snapped open, pouring copious tears. His pupils rolled back into his head. The whites of his eyes were stained dark with branching red veins. Harry was lost in his nightmares.

Kit sucked in a sharp breath, steeling himself, readying for the onslaught of power. He could do this. He sank his outstretched hand into the cold shadow. Power assaulted him, seeping into his pores, iced pins sliding through the skin, deep into the muscle. Gritting his teeth, Kit surrendered, letting it fill him. He shuddered and clenched his jaw, forcing his will to stop Harry taking control. He gasped and grunted as the magic sank deeper, into his blood, the very air he breathed. It was so strong. He'd never felt anything like it. How was Harry holding so much in every day?

This was not Harry imposing his will on Kit. It was the strength of his magic striking the edges of his mind, demanding entrance, desperate for the secrets of his soul. He saw fire. Felt its heat licking his flesh. Saw blood on his hands. Hands clawed at him, mouths devouring him. Losing himself, unable to move, unable to scream, unable to stop it. The screams of men, the ceaseless number of corpses piling at his feet.

No! Stop it!

He struggled against it, pushing it back, molding it, unsure how to translate its sheer raw energy. He couldn't hold it. He did the first thing that came to him, magic he had performed hundreds of times. He took the darkness and broke it down, simplifying its structure. It took everything Kit had. He fell to all fours, heaving, eyes screwed shut, spittle falling from his mouth in silent agony. It was too much. He screamed, releasing what he intended to be a strong gust of wind. Instead a great tempest erupted around him, circling him, growing until a great hurricane wind ripped through the small dwelling.

Chairs were thrown against the wall, barely missing him and Harry. Books were sent flying from their shelves. The pot above the fire was ripped from its hook and clattered loudly on the floor. Ash and charcoal blackened the air as it flew from the fireplace. The door burst open, banging loudly against its fame. The walls groaned. The chimney whistled, sending down great plumes of soot. The windows trembled in their frames, threatening to shatter. The walls creaked and protested. The ceiling rattled above their heads.

Kit threw himself atop Harry, waiting for the magic to wither. It seemed to last forever before the wind blew itself out and the shack's joints ceased to whine and pop. Kit was left deaf and staring about dumbly at the damage. "Holy fucking hell," Kit wheezed, trying to muster the strength to get up.

Harry moaned beneath him. Kit sat up to give him some space. Harry blinked. His eyes, honey brown once more, met Kit's. Through labored breaths and tearing eyes, he clutched at Kit's shirt, scrabbling to take hold of his arms, staring in amazement. He gasped, "You're here."

Kit stared at him quizzically. "Of course I am. You haven't gotten around to kicking me out yet."

"Don't leave me," Harry begged, his grip tightening.

Kit blinked, bewildered, but said softly, "I won't." He felt compelled to add when Harry's grip tightened, "I promise."

"Stay with me. Don't leave me alone again."

Kit pulled him into a gentle embrace, stroking the sweat-soaked hair off his hot forehead. "What do you mean?"

"Stay. Please, Louis. Don't leave me."

Tightness in Kit's chest constricted his breathing. But he didn't let go. He held Harry in his arms, cradling him even as pain settled over his heart. "I won't. I'll stay. As long as you need me."

"I'm sorry, Louis. I'm so sorry."

They stayed like that, with Harry clinging to a ghost, and Kit obliging him. He liked Harry's weight in his arms, enjoyed the intimacy even though it wasn't meant for him. Kit held onto that warmth as Harry fell into an uneasy sleep, grunting and mumbling every now and then, his eyelids restlessly twitching, but didn't wake screaming again.

It was too much of a struggle to replace Harry in his upset chair. Kit's body was still too delicate to bear both their weights. Attempting to make it upstairs to the bedroom was out of the question. Kit settled on leaning against the wall by the empty fireplace with Harry pressed against him. It was nowhere near comfortable, but Kit suffered it for Harry's uneasy peace.

* * * *

He woke with a crick in his neck, his legs aching, his ass numb and his arms empty. It was the hacking of an ax, becoming so familiar to Kit of late, that had awoken him with an uneasy start. Harry was hard at work. Dawn light was barely slithering in through the window, casting the room in a fiery amber glow, serving to warm Kit, even though his breath misted faintly before his face when he yawned.

His legs were taking revenge from being forced to lie on the floor under Harry's greater weight, profusely protesting when he tried to stand. A blanket fell from him as he stood, pooling around his feet. He squinted at it, realizing Harry must have wrapped him up. The room had been somewhat hastily repaired as well. Kit made it to Harry's righted chair, collapsed into it, taking in the sight of the woodsman and his secrets, burying his nightmares with each ax swing.

Harry's sleeves were rolled up to his elbows. Kit's heart kicked against his ribcage and his cock gave a lazy, misguided twitch at the sight of bulging, muscled flesh. Harry's right forearm tensed, ablaze with sweat reflecting the orange sunlight. His left was mottled red and white marble. He'd shied away from using it in front of Kit, but with each day, Harry seemed more willing to use it, though the strength and dexterity was obviously weaker.

Was that the source of his nightmares? Recalling the terror in Harry's screams helped soothe his morning arousal as he continued to watch.

He had to leave soon, but with each passing day, Kit felt less like saying goodbye. Not to the shack. Though he had to admit the rustic, quiet charm was growing on him. Losing the ability to run had scared him, driving him mad inside these four walls. But now, for the first time in more years than he could recall, Kit had stopped running. He could breathe, take in the sights.

Speaking of…

He refocused his attention on Harry, reliving that kiss before they'd been interrupted by Harry's magic, the dark power surging inside him.

Kit had experienced many forms of magic, but unlike the complete lack of control usually guiding him, forcing his body to comply, there had been a bizarre, intoxicating freedom Harry's brought with its raw unfettered power. He shuddered, recalling its unbridled strength.

Harry stopped to take a breath, his chest heaving. He rubbed and rotated his scarred arm. He winced with a pained grunt, the ax falling from his grip. He swore and kicked the log he'd been splitting. He took several deep breaths before sitting on a tree stump, slouched, forehead resting on his palm.

Kit got up and left the safety and seclusion of the hovel. He made his way over to Harry. Harry's head snapped up. His body tensed into a hard line as he watched Kit amble over. His expression was assessing, clinical. How much of last night did he recall?

"How're you feeling?" Harry asked in gruff tones before Kit could speak.

"I was going to ask you the same thing."

Harry deflected, "You're moving better."

So they weren't going to talk about last night. Kit played along. "All thanks to the attentive expertise of my doctor."

Harry's cheek twitched. "He's that good?"

The awkwardness cracked, but didn't crumble. Kit nudged it. "Yes, and I very much approve of his aftercare techniques."

"What do you mean?"

Kit smirked, unable to hold back his smile, and very slowly, but very deliberately bent low, his hands on Harry's shoulders to stop him stumbling, and pressed a soft kiss to Harry's mouth. He wanted Harry to know he wasn't afraid of him, that he trusted that Harry couldn't hurt him. His breath caught under Kit's touch, but he relaxed when Kit pulled back, smiling down at him. Harry's pained eyes tugged at Kit, leaving him a little disconcerted, but he wanted to make it better, to stop Harry's hurt. He pressed a smaller, soft kiss to the side of Harry's mouth, his thumb brushing his jawline.

"Kit," Harry protested weakly. "We shouldn't..."

Kit pulled away, making sure he hadn't gone too far. Harry's dark lashes cast heavy shadows over his cheeks. His lips parted a little, his breath warm on Kit's mouth. When his pale brown eyes swept up to meet Kit's, there was a question in his gaze, an endearing and heart-wrenching vulnerability. Harry closed his eyes and pressed forward. The kiss was soft, though not tentative.

They exchanged a few more easy kisses, Harry stroking Kit's stubble and Kit allowing his hand to explore the swirling scar tissue starting at Harry's collar and ending at his fingers. Harry tensed. Kit pulled back.

"Does it hurt?"

Harry peered at Kit's hand on his skin. "No. The damaged muscles are tight, but I need to use them to maintain maximum strength and function."

Kit pressed down gently, massaging the tight, scarred swirls. "What happened?"

"I got burned."

Kit chuffed and shook his head. "Really? I would never have guessed."

To his relief, Harry performed that half smile again.

"Was it the war?"

Harry looked down at his scarred arm, fingers curling into a fist. "No. After."

Kit knew he should stop, but didn't, wanting to know who had hurt this tender man. "The enemy?"

"No." Harry raised his hand and placed it softly over the brands marring Kit's skin as though it was the only place he had permission to touch. "It wasn't the enemy."

Kit took Harry's scarred hand and brought the mottled fingers to his mouth, kissing each knuckle softly. "It's the people we trust the most who hurt us the worst."

"Then I shouldn't trust you."

"Perhaps that would be wise." Kit placed Harry's hand on his throat, slowly sliding it down under his shirt. "I don't want to hurt you."

Staring into Kit's eyes, Harry splayed his fingers over Kit's chest. "I don't want to hurt you either."

Kit straightened a little, relieving some of the tightness around the brands. He took the chance to kiss Harry again, tilting Harry's face up to the sun. Lust was evident in the hard press of Harry's mouth, in the strength of his grip. There was also uncertainty in his furrowed brow. Kit gently stoked his thumb over the creases as though he could smooth them away.

"Come back into the house," Kit said, his lips still touching Harry's.

Harry dropped his gaze. Heart thudding painfully, Kit thought Harry would refuse. When he gave the smallest of nods, Kit released his held breath. Taking hold of Harry's hand, he hobbled back inside with Harry closely on his tail. Once the door was shut, Harry was on him, kissing him again, his hands tugging at Kit's coat. It fell to the floor, quickly followed by his shirt. Kit forced them to part and worked on undoing his trousers as he limped to the stairs. Kit was about to take his first step when Harry stopped him, sweeping away Kit's hair and pressing his lips to the nape of Kit's neck.

"Don't fight," was the only warning Kit got before Harry lifted him into his arms. Kit yelped in surprise, wrapping his arms around Harry's neck.

"Your arm," Kit protested.

"Your hip," Harry countered with a grunt. "I told you, I need to use my arm to strengthen the muscles."

"Still," Kit said, knowing he was no waif.

"Shut up." Harry grunted and kissed him again.

They made it up the stairs, Harry dropping Kit onto the bed delicately. "Was it worth it?" Kit asked, stroking the scarred arm in sympathy.

Harry lowered his body, pressing firmly against Kit. "Definitely."

Kit couldn't stop the jaw-breaking smile stretching over his face. "I'm glad." Harry leaned on his good arm, using the other to stroke Kit's hair off his forehead. Harry was watching him closely, staring into his eyes, at his nose, his mouth, the stubble on his jaw before locking their gazes once more. Kit returned his appreciative gaze, stroking his fingers through Harry's beard, drawing along the line of his lips.

"Kiss me," Kit begged, never getting enough of the bristly press and soft exploration.

Kit's pale skin had taken on a delightful warm blush, his blue eyes were shining. Harry could deny him nothing in that moment. He leaned down and opened his mouth to Kit. Kit groaned beneath him, a deep thundering noise coming from his chest. Heat traveled from Harry's chest to his cock.

Kit was a criminal, wanted by the Blue Crows. He was injured and in Harry's care. His mere presence woke the darkness inside Harry. It should all have been enough to warn Harry this was a dangerous mistake. But Kit's company filled Harry's empty heart with a thrilling excitement he had not felt in a long time, something he'd thought he would never feel again. No, this was something new, something Harry daren't explore, scared he'd hunger for it once Kit was healed and gone from his life. But for now, in this moment, he allowed himself to be taken in by Kit's coaxing warmth and beauty.

Harry kissed him until they were both breathless. Keeping his mouth and nose pressed against Kit's skin, he worked his way down the smaller man's body. He traced Kit's collarbone with his tongue, licking and kissing a path to his stiff nipples, lapping and sucking them. Kit moaned and arched up, his mouth open, his hand combing through Harry's hair, holding him in place. Harry's fingers found and traced the faint patchwork of bruises on Kit's skin.

"Does it hurt?"

Kit breathed, "Only a little. Don't stop, Dr. Woodsman."

Harry shook his head, smiling, and bit at Kit's ribs. Kit's back arched again. Harry took the chance to pull down Kit's trousers, Kit's cock jutting and slapping his belly once free. Harry left a wet trail down Kit's stomach, his nose tickled by the dark golden hair leading to Kit's pubis. He breathed in deeply and took Kit's hard cock in hand, pumping slowly. Kit gasped again. Harry smirked and kissed the base, tongue lapping at his balls.

Kit squirmed. "Ah! Your beard." His words were buried under a deep growl.

Harry did it again. Kit groaned. His stomach muscles tensed into beautiful solid ridges. Harry stroked his hand along Kit's inner thigh. Kit's legs opened up to him. He squirmed again. "Harry... please..."

Harry licked the tip of Kit's cock, tasting the salty dew gathering at his piss slit. It flexed in his hand. Kit hissed through his teeth. Harry kissed the crown, the ring of his lips widening, taking in more and more until the full length was resting against his tongue, tip pressing the back of his throat. Kit was watching him, eyes tearing, golden hair mussed, cheeks glowing. "My God," he gasped around a wide smile. "What are you doing to me?"

Harry relented. He pulled away, almost releasing Kit before plunging back down. He worked his mouth around Kit, taking him in as far as he could, over and over. Kit was calling out filthy curses. Harry didn't stop, using his tongue and lips until Kit was bucking off the bed, his fingers tightening into a fist in Harry's hair. "Harry... Stop... So close." Even as he spoke, Kit fucked Harry's mouth, his hips grinding off the bed, humping into Harry's mouth. He yelped and grunted as spurt after spurt of his seed hit the back of Harry's throat. Spasms shook his body. His cock flexed against Harry's tongue as he sucked out the last drops of Kit's release, his tongue cleaning his foreskin and lapping his shaft. Kit trembled at every wet touch.

Harry released him slowly, swallowing every drop, savoring the soft press of velvet skin against his tongue. Kit lay lifeless, eyes closed, his blood-flushed chest heaving. Harry crawled up his body, kissing his sweat-shiny skin as he went. Kit moaned at each touch of his lips, gathering Harry into his arms and kissing him soundly between breathless gasps. "My God," he managed after a few deep breaths. "No one's ever... That was glorious." He closed his eyes and pressed his forehead to Harry's. "Thank you."

Harry laughed, a little breathless himself. "You're welcome."

Kit gave an airless chuckle and stroked his fingers through Harry's hair. His hands traveled over Harry's shoulders and back, his nails scratching lightly along his shoulder blades and down his spine. His hands cupped and squeezed Harry's ass. "Where did you learn that?"

"You pick up a few things as an army doctor."

"Oh, I can imagine." His fingers stroked teasingly under Harry's trousers. "You're furry all over. I like it." His hand slipped around and cupped Harry's balls, fingers teasing the sensitive patch of skin behind them. "Here too." Wrapping his hand around Harry's cock, Kit kissed him again.

Harry grunted and pressed into Kit's touch. Kit's grip tightened. It had been so long. After the war, after Louis, he had not sought out the company of other men, as though he were being unfaithful to what they had shared. He felt it now, but desire for release overtook him, his body twisting into a tight spring as the ridges of Kit's callused palm and fingers pumped the heat to the surface, fire spreading through his body, drawing him away from the cold ghost of lost love. He clutched at Kit, rutting against him, pressing his lips to Kit's mouth, his cheek, his jaw, his throat, inhaling the woody scent and sweaty musk.

Kit changed his grip. Harry swallowed his cry, biting into the meat of Kit's shoulder. Kit worked his fist faster, his other hand still groping at Harry's ass, spreading it, his fingers stroking close to his exposed entrance, teasing. Harry gulped, the sensation not completely strange to him, but it had been a long time. He eased into it nonetheless, squirming as he felt his release rushing through him. His balls tightened. He found Kit's mouth again, sucking on his tongue and lips until his orgasm crashed through him.

Light blinded him, ecstasy taking him to a higher plane where he had no other sense but touch, his skin alive and tingling, pleasure erupting through every nerve. He came with a long groan, thrusting into Kit's fist, painting his hand and stomach with wet, white threads. He grunted and rutted and groaned aloud, sure he must have deafened Kit. He sank back onto the bed, inside Kit's warm embrace, contentment covering him like a soft blanket.

Kit was kissing his temple and stroking his clean hand through Harry's hair.

Harry settled beside him, pulling a blanket around them and muttering, "Thank you."

He fell asleep after hearing Kit's responding chuckle and whispered, "You're welcome."

* * * *

"How can I help?"

Harry glanced up from stripping bark from the trunk of a birch. He had in mind to make a small dining table for the main room.

Kit stood over him, stubbornly not using his cane, hand on his uninjured hip and his perpetual smile on his lips.

"You're still injured."

"It wasn't a problem yesterday." Kit smirked. "Or this morning."

Harry found himself grinning back. As soon as Kit had opened his eyes, Harry had clung to him, grinding against him, taking their hard cocks in hand, pumping them together, bringing them to lazy, comfortable completion.

"Come on," Kit persisted. "Let me help, teach me the ways of the woodsman. I already have the beard for it."

Harry shook his head, an irrepressible smile tugging at his mouth, but it was true. Golden bristles caught in the morning sun's light. "Very well, come here." He rolled a thick log alongside the trunk he'd been stripping and gestured for Kit to sit. He spent some time teaching Kit how to strip the bark. It wasn't complicated, and Harry was sure Kit would grow bored soon enough. But Kit learned quickly, happily continuing where Harry had started, leaving Harry to move on to patching up a leak in the roof. The result, he'd been told, of his latest episode and Kit's attempt to fight off the darkness.

They had not spoken much of that night. Kit hadn't asked and Harry could not bring himself to explain, feeling the utter cad for mistaking Kit for Louis. It had come back to him once he'd woken in Kit's arms, and after rearranging some of the house, he'd retreated into his work, unsure how to even look Kit in the eye. But Kit had been unafraid, soothing Harry's fear.

Kit was not Louis. The differences were so clear now they could not even be called cousins if stood side by side. But in that moment, trapped in his memories, Harry had clung to his imagined version of Louis, the one that came to him when he called, the one that comforted him when he needed it. But that was not Louis.

After a few hours of silent work, Kit called from inside the house, "Food's ready."

Harry examined his patch job. It would do for another winter, but the roof was old and would probably need completely replacing. It would be a big job and was not one he was looking forward to doing alone.

"Hurry up. It's getting cold," Kit shouted.

Smiling at Kit's growing pride and enthusiasm at playing house, unsure if he noticed it, Harry dropped his tools to the earth before following them down. Kit greeted him with a steaming bowl in each hand and a hunk of crusty brown bread under his arm, limping stiffly without his cane. "Shall we eat out here?"

Harry took his bowl. It was strange how quickly they had fallen into this bizarre domesticity. He wanted to kiss Kit, so he did. Kit was smiling when Harry pulled back. "What do I get when I master sanding?"

"I wouldn't say you've mastered stripping bark."

Kit laughed. "Well, one can't be good at everything. I'll gladly leave the stripping to you. I do have other talents." Harry stepped closer, but Kit held up a hand. "But right now I need to eat. Between you and working after a week of lying about, I'm positively drained."

Still smiling, Harry took the offered bowl. Their fingers touched. Kit flinched and the bowl slipped from his grip. Harry hissed as hot broth splashed his trouser legs.

Kit was stiff as a board and staring over Harry's shoulder. He grasped Harry's wrist to stop him turning. He was shaking. "There's someone coming." His wide blue eyes appeared colorless in the sun's glow.

Harry gripped Kit's hand. "What do they look like?" He managed to keep his voice steady. "Kit? Tell me."

"A man. With a horse and cart."

"His clothes?"

"I — " Kit's eyes were huge, all color drained from his face.

"Is he wearing armor?"

"No."

"How old?"

"Old."

Harry sighed. "Is he wearing a big floppy hat?"

Kit's eyes flicked to Harry, some of the tension in his shoulders easing, his eyes less feral. "Yes."

"Don't worry. Kit, look at me. He's from the village. Take the food inside and wait for me."

"But—"

"Kit," Harry said more firmly. "Do as I say."

Kit wasn't happy, but did as told.

"Slowly," Harry said as Kit attempted to rush. "It's fine. Don't panic."

Kit nodded and calmly disappeared into the cottage. Harry casually cleared away his tools until the man stepped onto his land and called out, "Hello there."

Harry approached the old man. "Hello, Francis. Isn't it too soon for you to be back on your feet?"

"Bah! Don't you start, Doc. You're as bad as Celeste. Man has to work."

Harry shook his head, but knew a lost cause when he heard one. "What can I do you for?"

"Depends what you have for me and what you need."

Harry forced a smile. "I've some aged venison and a brace of wood pigeons."

Francis raised a bushy brow. "Slim pickings."

Harry grunted. He didn't admit he was sharing his supplies with his recent guest.

"Any news?" Harry asked as he led Francis to his storage shed.

"Amy Faro's fat as a tick. Due any day now, I reckon. Paula Jenks' hip's giving her jip as usual. Young Freddy More's been tussling with the Tillow lads, few scrapes and a broken nose."

Harry nodded, knowing he should probably go back to the village with Francis. He'd been neglecting his duties as unofficial village doctor. There were plenty of experienced women in the village to serve as midwife, but Amy had lost her last baby and he didn't want to risk her losing a second when he could have been there to help.

They bartered and settled on a good price. Harry exchanged his meat and some timber for some tinned and dry goods he could store for the leaner months. It was only when he was loading the last plank and Francis was helping him secure a canvas over them that Francis gestured to the cottage with a jut of his chin and said, "Who's your friend?"

Harry tensed then cleared his throat, giving an answer as close to the truth as possible. "A patient."

Francis must have read something in his face. He beamed, a knowing smile on his lips. The old man saw too much. "Not like you to take on a live-in patient." When Harry didn't reply, Francis patted the stacked timber and he said with a grin, "I see. Good to know you're not alone out here, lad."

Harry took the chance to change the subject. "Lad?"

"You are to me." Francis huffed as he climbed into his seat, replacing his giant hat. "You coming back with me this time round?"

Harry flicked his gaze to the house. He and Kit had been surviving on what Harry could hunt or scavenge from the forest. Kit could do with some clothes other than his ruined suit and Harry's castoffs. "Give me a minute," he said and made his way back to the house.

Chapter Six

Riding on the back of the rickety cart was not the most comfortable way to travel, as it swayed and bounced along the trodden path cutting its way through forest and fields. It was also cramped sitting between the merchant's goods and Harry, who took up more than his fair share of the limited seating space. Though Kit had to admit it was nice to have an excuse to press against his solid bulk. At one point the wheel had bucked the back end of the cart so high Kit would have been thrown overboard were it not for Harry pulling him back. He'd left his arm around Kit's waist, and an anchoring grip on Kit's shirt. Kit had given him a wry smile and Harry's cheeks had flushed a little. He'd averted his gaze for the rest of the journey.

The village of Paix came into view and Kit experienced an excited and equally apprehensive jolt through his chest. He took in the small, disorganized spread of pale cob buildings and thatched roofs, smelled the smoke of chimneys and the briny air coming from the river running alongside it, which fed off the Rashivim Sea. People were dotted about, walking in that dithering way so far removed from the rushed march of city folk. That same jolt ignited Kit and had him pressing farther into Harry while trying to get a better look.

"Excited?" Harry asked with a smile.

"Thrilled," Kit answered with forced hauteur, struggling to remain stoic.

Harry shook his head. His hand moved to rub Kit's biceps. He leaned in close to say, "Don't worry. No one here will bother you."

Heat crawled up Kit's face. Harry read him so easily. It was disconcerting, but his heart warmed under Harry's concern. He smiled, and had opened his mouth to offer a scathing retort when a voice boomed too loud in the calm serenity. "Dr. Tallis, good to see you, son."

Harry jumped from the cart to clasp hands with an aged, rotund gentleman wearing what would have been a fancy suit at one time, but was now patched and had been upturned so many times, Kit could almost see the tops of his boots. The sleeves of his jacket were also rolled up around his meaty arms. He was bald, but made up for it with thick whiskers, reminding Kit of a walrus.

"Good to see you, Thom."

"And who's this?" He gestured to Kit with an openly friendly if overly surprised smile.

Kit tensed despite his best efforts and offered a neutral smile in response.

"This is Kit, a friend and patient."

"From your army days?"

Kit saw the effort it took for Harry to lie to this man. "Yes."

Thom looked Kit up and down once he'd disembarked a little stiffly from the cart, trying not to wince. Thom beamed and clapped Kit on the shoulder so hard his knees buckled. "Wonderful to meet you, lad. I'm Thomas Moorland, owner of the Dusty Swan."

Kit nodded, shaking the man's hand. "Nice to meet you."

Turning back to Harry, Moorland said, "Come for a drink when you're done doing the rounds. So," he said, laughing, "that might be some time tomorrow evening with the queue you're going to draw."

Harry offered a smile. "Will do. Thanks, Thom."

"Least I can do, Doc."

With a final clap on Harry's back, Moorland departed.

"You're certainly popular," Kit said.

Harry merely grunted.

They walked down the windy street after thanking Francis for the ride, Harry setting a slow pace Kit suspected was for his sake. They went to a bakery first, and Kit was nearly bowled over by the loud, warm greeting Harry received. The baker, one Ms. Fogel, came from the kitchen after hearing the squeal of joy from the girl at the counter, and upon seeing Harry threw her arms around him, dusting his coat with a liberal amount of flour. Harry asked after the rest of the Fogel clan, discussing some ailment or other, but Kit was too withdrawn to pay much attention to the details, blending as much as possible into the background. They asked after his presence, but once Harry had made introductions Kit was mostly forgotten, which he encouraged. Harry was the main attraction. They left with a basket of free bread and pastries, both women blushing rosily in their wake.

Harry had tried to gently rebuff their generosity, but the women had insisted, shoving the wrapped parcels at him until he was forced to take them.

It wasn't just the bakery. At every building they passed someone came out to greet Harry with warm welcomes and free goods, some dragging him in to discuss their health. At one establishment, presumably a fishmonger's, judging by the smell, Kit had to wait outside while Harry dealt with a boil that needed lancing.

And so it continued until Kit was left holding baskets and bags filled with various goodies as Harry went to each resident requiring his aid. Kit had been furnished with some new clothes, homespun and a little ill-fitting, but he didn't think the kind residents letting him have them for an exceedingly low price would appreciate his true opinion. So he smiled and took them with heartfelt thanks, a little peeved at the younger cut and color of his knee-length britches and pale flouncy shirt, despite his recently acquired beard. All he forgave though when he met the appraising up-and-down gaze Harry gave him. He wasn't accustomed to blushing so readily, but Harry seemed to bring it out in him.

At least he now possessed a decent pair of boots, which fit surprisingly well and added a certain maturity to the look. He was sad to give up Harry's coat for the very fine, if much-worn leather and fur-lined number the fishmonger's son had offered in exchange for the lanced boil. Harry had assured him the smell wouldn't linger forever. For now it was tucked away in one of the bags.

Leaning against the latest house Harry had disappeared into, Kit dropped the array of gifts to the floor. Half-hidden in the shade of overhanging ivy crawling up the side of the building, he breathed in the sun-warmed dust and picked at the embroidered cuff of his new shirt.

He should never have agreed to come here with Harry. With each patient Harry tended to, with every smiling welcome he received, Kit felt the distance between them growing.

Harry was not like him. He had a life and a purpose and people who depended on him. Whatever he had suffered, he had moved on, finding a place for himself. Did Kit resent him for that? It was ugly and selfish and left Kit sickened at his own inability to be happy for the man he cared about. He shivered despite the warm air, folding his arms, hugging his tight chest.

Harry was only on the other side of that door, but he may as well have been hundreds of miles out of Kit's reach. Kit was a patient, a bump in the road, a burden. What was worse, he was a danger, something that should have never dared intrude on Harry and his peaceful life. What would happen to this small community if they lost Harry? Kit had no right to interfere, no right to want more from Harry, to expect...

He smiled, chiding himself. He should have learned to never expect more.

It was time to leave.

Pushing off from the wall, he was about to go and tell Harry he'd meet him somewhere later. It would give Kit time to get far enough away while Harry was still busy, until it was too late for Harry to go searching for him. Harry would try to stop him if he knew Kit's true intentions.

Kit stopped when he noticed a young lad pelting it up the street, kicking up dust and aiming straight for him. Kit tensed, ready to…what? Fight? The young man reached the house and banged on the door hard enough to rattle its hinges, his eyes wide and frantic. Kit grabbed his arm. "What are you doing?"

The lad looked at him, shocked and flustered. "Who are you? Let go. I need Dr. Tallis." He banged on the door with his other arm, shouting for Harry.

Kit released him, unsure why he'd grabbed him in the first place. Being in this peaceful place, surrounded by strangers out in the open, had Kit on edge. This lad wasn't an enemy. He needed Harry's help.

The door opened and Harry filled the doorframe. "What going on? Davy? Is it—"

"It's Amy."

Without further explanation, Harry was off and running, at first being led by the lad, but he soon overtook him, clearly knowing the way. Abandoning the array of gifts, Kit started to follow after, but stopped.

Go, now.

But a second later he was hobbling as quickly as he could, heading in the direction Harry had fled. He lost sight of them, but knew the house by the open door and the young woman being led out by another, her hands and skirt soaked with blood. Again Kit paused, heart thumping.

"Poor Miss Amy," the young girl said, visibly shaking in the other woman's arms. "I've never seen so much blood. I didn't—" She burst into tears and the other woman tried to soothe her.

"You did the right thing, sending Davy to fetch the doctor. She's in good hands now." She led the girl to a water pump to wash her hands.

Kit looked to the house, to the open door, the interior untouched by the sun—ominous. A scream sent his heart jolting as he trod inside, unobstructed by anyone. The house was simple, but a little more ornate and comfortable than Harry's, the wooden furniture polished, the spread of knick-knacks lending it a personal touch and the scents of cooking and a certain cologne giving the place its unique, lived-in aroma.

He followed the wails, which lead him upstairs, climbing slowly not because of the pain in his hip but because of his own fear at what he'd see once he reached the top. He heard Harry's voice under the shrieks, but Kit couldn't discern their meaning.

Reaching the room where the cries of pain were emanating from, Kit peered in and immediately wished he hadn't. The screaming, now quieted to moaning sobs, came from a young, very distressed woman, curly hair disarrayed over her pillow, sweat glistening on her pale skin, face screwed-up in pain. The young man, Davy, knelt by her bed, hand held in her crushing grip, pushing the wet strands of hair from her wet face and whispering something in her ear.

The girl had been right. There was a lot of blood, more blood than Kit, in his limited experience, thought there ought to be during childbirth, but what did he know?

Harry knelt on the floor, back hunched over. Kit took a step into the room, unsure what drove him to do so.

"Who are you? What are you doing in here?" A matronly woman with a shrewd uncompromising scowl walked up to Kit, a swaddled baby in one arm. "Get out of here this instant." She shooed him as if he were a mangy dog that'd wandered into her kitchen off the street.

"Harry," he said, ignoring her red-faced outrage.

Harry didn't respond, muttering to himself, leaning over farther. Kit took another step closer, ignoring the angry midwife, fearing what he'd see. A pale, tiny infant lay lifeless on a bed of soiled blankets, blood and other fluids staining its pale skin. Blue skin. Its thin eyelids were shut, its tiny lips open in a silent cry. Kit swallowed and watched as Harry pumped its little chest, the violence against the delicate ribcage almost too difficult to witness, but what was worse was the fierce determination set on Harry's face, his mouth set in a grimacing snarl as he counted before stopping to breathe into that tiny mute mouth. The child's chest inflating with Harry's breath had Kit's heart aching.

"Come on," Harry muttered through gritted teeth, his compressions never ceasing. "Come on, little one. Don't give up."

Kit held his breath, the distant cries of the baby's distraught mother ripping into him.

Come one, come on, come on. Please.

Harry filled the tiny lungs with air, stopped to listen for life. The compressions continued. The baby didn't stir. Its eyes didn't flutter. It didn't scream in outrage at its violent welcome into the world.

"Come on now, little one. Come on," Harry chanted, pleading.

Kit couldn't stand it. He went to Harry, placing a hand on Harry's arm, which still fought to bring the child back. "Harry." Kit's voice cracked and Harry didn't hear him. He cleared the lump from his throat. "Harry, you have to stop now."

The mother gave a choked whimper and pulled Davy closer, burying her face against his chest.

Harry shrugged off Kit's touch and carried on, breathing air into the limp little body once more.

"Harry, please, you can't—"

A soft cry cut Kit off. He stepped back, scared to hope. The cry grew louder until a full-blown wail assaulted the air.

Harry took the tiny infant into his arms, cradling it close, rubbing color back into its skin. "There we go. That wasn't so hard, was it?"

Kit stared in awe and fell to his knees. Harry turned to him, his teary smile constricting Kit's heart. The child continued to scream, and it was the most wonderful sound Kit had ever heard. He reached out and touched the baby's almost too soft, pale cheek, feeling unworthy of witnessing such a miracle. He looked to Harry and found him smiling back, slack-jawed and dumb.

"Doc? Is he…" Davy was at his side, his cheeks wet with tears, hands shaking as he reached out for his child.

"He is," Harry said, passing the new life to his father for inspection.

Davy gasped in awe and burst into full-fledged tears before standing and taking the boy to see his mother, introducing them for the first time.

"Oh, Davy, he's…" Words failed her as Davy pressed the newborn into her exhausted arms, his hands never fully letting go as the baby quieted down to feed for the first time, while his parents sobbed.

"Mrs. Carmac, could you introduce the little lad to his big sister?"

Mrs. Carmac, the serious woman holding the other baby, stared open-mouthed then nodded absently, resting the bundled baby girl alongside her brother.

"Thank you, Doctor," the girl sobbed from the bed. "Thank you so much."

* * * *

Sitting at the edge of the bar, leaning against the wall, Harry had closed his eyes, lulled by the tune played on the piano in the far corner. He was almost dozing off when Thom placed two tankards in front of him and Kit. He sat up with a jolt. "Thanks, Thom. How much do I owe you?"

"For what you did for young Amy? On the house. God damned miracle worker, that's what you are."

Harry shook his head, but was too tired to argue. It had been a long day. So long in fact, Thom had offered him and Kit a room for the night above the pub.

"You really are," Kit said when Thom moved off to serve someone else.

"I'm not," Harry said, his exhaustion dulling the sharp edge in his words. He was already on his fourth drink, as the whole village had come together to celebrate the birth of David Junior and Henrietta, named after Harry.

"I didn't know you were a Henry," Kit said.

Harry grunted and took a healthy pull on his cider, uncomfortable with the flocks of attention and congratulations which had finally quietened. Kit eyed him curiously. Harry wanted to reach out and touch him. He might have done were they back at the cabin, but he didn't want to cause Thom any trouble. Miracle worker or not, there were still laws. He settled on meeting Kit's gaze.

"Why do you live so far from the village? It's obvious you're important to these people."

Harry swallowed and shook his head. "Too dangerous. The…" He didn't want to mention the darkness, as though saying it out loud would pollute the air. He flexed his burned hand and Kit tracked the movement.

"So," Thom said, making Kit visibly jump, "where you from, young Kit? Don't recognize your accent."

Harry sobered quickly as Kit tensed. But he smiled and said easily, "Rasacara."

"Really?" Thom said, awed.

"Will that be a problem?" Kit asked amicably.

"Bah! What do I care? War's been over years. We've got folk from every corner of the empire settled here. Years ago, this place was part of a huge port town, but even long before the war, trade routes had changed to bigger settlements. We're descended from what was left behind."

Kit cast a quick glance around the pub.

"So you two met in the army?" Thom asked easily.

"Thom," Harry warned him off gently.

Thom held up his hands, glass in one, cloth in the other. "Don't mind me, old man's curiosity. It was a bloody long war. Surprised anyone one made it out alive. If it weren't for what happened in Rasacara…" He trailed off, giving Kit an apologetic grimace. He cleared his throat. "Though, of course, I'd long since retired before the last campaign."

"Lucky you," Kit muttered into his drink.

Thom dropped the subject and moved off to serve another patron.

Kit and Harry sat in silence for a time, the air thick between them.

"You're from Rasacara."

"Yes."

"You don't look—"

"Half-breed. Or so I've been told." Kit looked to him. "I did not serve in the Rasacaran army. I was very much on your side."

The Blue Crows, of course. They recruited witches from all over the empire, seeking out any magical talent. Heritage or creed didn't matter to the Witch Army. Rasacara was no place for witches. A culture that thrived on invention and machines, they believed magic to be barbaric and corrupt. Harry could see why.

"When were you recruited?"

"Like most, as a child. Don't make that face," he said when he caught Harry's scowl. He couldn't help it, imagining being taking from your home and family and thrust into a world of fighting. "It could have been worse," Kit said as though reading Harry's mind. "I went from being a poor street stray to someone important, to the Crows at least. I was fed and had a roof over my head. It was more than someone like me could have dreamed of."

Even as Kit spoke, his words were tinted with grief, his eyes drawn in a far-off stare. He cleared his throat and stood. "Enough reminiscing about the good old days." He sighed then tried to stifle a yawn.

"Let's go to bed," Harry said.

Kit eyed him, uncertainty tainting his haughty brow. "What about your party? You're the hero. You can't abandon your admirers."

Harry couldn't pinpoint what was unsettling Kit. Perhaps it was the new surroundings and strange people, or maybe he was a little traumatized after witnessing the birth, but Harry doubted it. Kit struck him as a man who had seen and suffered much worse. Something had changed since they'd reached the village.

"I'm exhausted. And besides…" He looked over the rest of the pub, at the swaying band of patrons who started singing as the pianist began another song. Harry smiled. "I don't think anyone will notice."

Kit nodded and gave his own sad smile. Harry helped him off the bar stool, knowing full well Kit was capable, but not wanting to miss the chance to take his hand. He placed an arm around Kit's waist and left it there until they were in their room.

Harry took Kit to bed. They kissed as they shed a layer of clothing, kicking off their boots, neither of them letting go of the other for long. Kit lay atop Harry, pressing gentle kisses to his mouth. It was nice, simple, as though they shared these sorts of kisses all the time, undemanding, simply wanting to touch and be touched. Kit pulled back and stared down at Harry, that sad look in his eyes again.

"What's wrong?" Harry asked in such hushed tones he was unsure if Kit heard him.

"Nothing." It was a lie, but Kit got back to kissing him, his mouth a little more possessive and demanding.

As much as Harry was enjoying the attention, his eyelids grew heavy and his lips tired.

"Harry?"

He grunted, eyes closed.

He heard a huff of laughter from Kit and wanted to apologize. He was just so tired.

"It's all right. Go to sleep. You've had a long day, Dr. Woodsman."

He wanted to kiss Kit again in gratitude, but he couldn't summon the energy. He fell asleep with Kit's warm weight pressing against him.

* * * *

Francis offered them a ride home, even though he wasn't due to head out for another week, and Kit was grateful. Their bags and all the thank-you gifts Harry had received were already packed onto the cart by the time Kit finished the breakfast Harry had fetched them — smoked fish and poached eggs.

Harry was in a lively mood. Perhaps that was what saving lives did to you. Kit could only guess. Harry performed a few more checks around the village and went to see Amy and her brood before returning with a contagious smile on his face. Kit had wanted to kiss him, but restrained himself.

They were going back to the shack. Kit felt like a villain, as though he were pulling Harry from the circle of happiness and friendly faces. He knew it wasn't true. Harry had preferred isolation long before Kit had intruded on his life. But he couldn't help feeling Harry was cutting this visit short on his behalf. Selfishly, Kit was glad to be returning, wanting Harry to himself, wanting to touch him without thinking about how many eyes were on them.

Harry gave his final farewells and they sat a little more comfortably between the food and various other gifts on the cart. They weren't touching. Kit kept his eyes on the road. Silence fell between them for most the journey, Harry managing to doze off as the cart bounced and swayed on the uneven path through the landscape.

Kit watched, a faint smile shaping his mouth when Harry began to snore.

Just a little bit longer.. He only wanted a little bit more time before he had to say goodbye — or before he was forced to.

"What's the matter?" Harry asked when he woke, catching Kit watching him. His voice was rough with sleep and he squinted as the sun dappled through the tree canopy.

"Nothing," Kit answered automatically.

"Is it the brand?"

Kit smiled to reassure him. "No. It's been tended to most thoroughly."

"But there's something."

Kit looked away, pretending to be distracted by new buds of blossoms appearing on some of the trees. This part of the forest would be wonderful once spring fully settled in. Shame he wouldn't see it.

"Was it too much? Going to the village?"

"No," Kit said. Was that a lie? Had he lost his faith in men so completely he could no longer be around others without growing anxious? Then he saw that tiny baby in Harry's arms, the thankful sobs of a mother and father. Perhaps not, not completely. "I'm glad I came with you." *Glad to know you're happy.*

Harry reached out and entwined their fingers on the cart bed. "So am I."

They fell into a more comfortable silence as the cart bounced along, Kit struggling to breathe as his heart constricted. He tightened his grip on Harry's hand. He didn't want this to end, didn't want to lose Harry's touch. He pretended to sleep the rest of the journey, stopping Harry's questions. He leaned against Harry, listening to his steady heartbeat.

Chapter Seven

It was late afternoon by the time they reached the shack. Francis bade them farewell once they'd unloaded the cart. Once inside, Kit was stopped by Harry taking hold of his wrist. He didn't fight when Harry pulled him against his chest, wrapping his arms around Kit's back and nuzzling into his neck, breathing deeply. Kit wanted to hold him in return, encase him in strength and warmth, sharing every breath.

"I think it's time I leave."

Harry tensed, the length of his body locking up. After a long moment he said, "I see."

Kit moved out of the circle of Harry's arms, forcing a smile, heart deflating. He was disappointed Harry hadn't argued. He dipped in into a theatrical bow, unable to look Harry in the eye as he said, "Thank you for your hospitality, Dr. Woodsman. I will always be in your debt."

He felt Harry's gaze, unwavering and assessing.

Let me go. Forget about me. Kit swallowed, closing his eyes against the throb of pain in his heart.

"Kit." Harry took his hand, pulling him straight and stroking his jaw, forcing their eyes to meet. Hurt shone through Harry's amber eyes, his lips set in a grim line, his brows creased in pain. "Stay," he said softly.

Kit's breath caught. God, how much he wanted to. To give in and hide away with Harry forever. He'd never felt this before, the enormity of it almost crushed him. He had to look away.

"No," he said, voice breaking as he fought against the bands tightening around his chest. "I can't."

Harry stepped close once more, his scent engulfing Kit. Kit's breath caught. Harry stroked the line of Kit's jaw, scratching at the bristle, forcing Kit to look at him again. The hope in that gaze was too much for Kit to bear.

He couldn't do this.

Kit met Harry's advance, lips inches apart. Lowering his eyelids, he watched Harry's lips, saw the trap opening for him. Summoning a sneer from deep down, he said, "How pathetic."

Harry froze. "What?"

Kit smiled. It hurt, but he endured. "I said, you're pathetic." Into Harry's astonished silence he said, "Who do you see when you look at me, when you fuck me?"

Harry took a sharp step back, looking at Kit like he was stranger. Kit didn't let him retreat, closing the space.

"What was he called, the one you called out for? Louis, wasn't it?"

Kit saw the words hit Harry. He recoiled, but Kit didn't let him escape, moving into his space again.

"Don't say his name."

The bitter stab of jealousy stung, tightening Kit's throat, but he couldn't stop, couldn't help twisting the knife a little more. "Do we look so alike? Is that why you took me in?"

"Don't," Harry warned.

"Is that why you helped me? Touched me?" He gave a scornful laugh. "Did I measure up? Did I make a decent substitute?"

"Stop."

Harry's pain was so raw, so close to the surface, his disappointment like a blade to the gut, yet Kit kept picking at the wound until it bled anew. He laughed shakily. "What happened? Did he break your heart? Did he leave you? I'm not surprised if your feelings are so easily transferable."

Harry was on him in a second, backing him into the wall, his hand on Kit's throat, firm but not tight, his eyes ablaze. "Stop it, Kit." He was angry, but there was a desperate edge to his voice.

Kit shuddered, his breath shaky, but knew Harry wouldn't hurt him. He had to try harder, reach further into Harry's heart and tear it apart, tearing his own in the process. "Don't worry. I can help. I'll make you forget all about him." Kit felt a small part of himself crumble, the small piece of self-respect he'd managed to scrape together. He lowered his voice, his hand slipping between their bodies, fingers groping Harry through his trousers. "You can do what you want with me. Fuck me. Tear me apart. Pretend I'm him. Pretend I'm Louis."

Harry growled. He grabbed Kit's wrists and slammed them into the wall. Kit saw the urge to hit him flash in Harry's eyes, saw the restraint it took. Pain rippled through Kit's bones. It was sharp and affirming. Harry saw someone else when he looked at him, longed for someone else, and Kit fucking hated it.

"You're not..." Harry's voice shook. His grip loosened but he didn't let go. "At first... When I first saw you, you bore some resemblance to Louis." His voice strained on the name, like he'd taken a blow to the throat. "But you're not him."

Kit's chest swelled, pain rippling out with each beat of his heart, but he wouldn't show it. Harry wished he were here, wished Louis were here instead of Kit. He glared up at Harry, dying a little with every passing second.

Harry's brows knitted. He looked so tired, so angry and broken. Kit had done that. He startled when instead of unleashing his fury, Harry sighed and leaned forward, pressing his forehead to Kit's shoulder. When Harry spoke, his voice was low with controlled calm. "I helped you because you were hurt, because I'm not a complete bastard, because I know exactly what the Crows are capable of. I want you to stay because... I..."

Kit couldn't stand to hear him struggle, didn't want to hear vows or promises, even though he'd forced Harry into this position. Rage and pain he could deal with. They were old, reliable weapons his master had taught him to exploit. But now he felt dirty, the stink of his past clinging to his skin, infecting Harry.

This was it. This was the end.

Harry pulled back, his face startlingly neutral, as though he'd resigned himself to whatever decision Kit made. "If you want to leave, go. I won't stop you."

Kit swallowed hard, fighting the burn behind his eyes.

Harry took a farther step back, meeting Kit's eyes. "You can push me away, hurt me as much as you want, but I know you're scared shitless of going out that door. But I don't know if it's the Crows you fear or admitting you want to be with me, that you want to stop running."

Rage hit Kit in a rush. "Fuck you!" He fought against Harry's hold and Harry released him. "Fuck you. You have no idea what you're talking about. You don't know anything about me, what I've done, what I'm capable of—" He drew a shuddering breath as his words faltered. "I'm doing this to protect you, you bastard."

Harry chuffed grimly, not rising to meet Kit's rage. "But who protects you?"

Kit blinked at him, frozen.

Harry's soft brown gaze lowered as moved away from Kit. Fists clenched, he went to the staircase. His footfalls were heavy and slow as he thudded up the stairs.

The heat of his body—reassuring, safe—dissipated, leaving Kit cold. He sagged against the wall, throat bobbing as he swallowed. Shaking, he buried his face in his hands, fighting the churning in his gut. Waiting for his heart to calm down, he looked to the door.

Harry was right. He was scared shitless. He'd nearly lost his last battle with the Crows and was in no better shape to defend himself. But he was also terrified of Harry one day seeing him for what he truly was and realizing what a huge mistake he'd made. Abandoned by his master, it had taken a long time for Kit to pick up the shattered parts of his life and reshape them. He didn't think he was strong enough to do it a second time.

He straightened, ignoring the lingering throb of pain from the brand. He made it to the door, shaking harder with each step, and reached out, fingertips grazing the smooth wood. He flinched back as though burned. He couldn't do it, couldn't leave it like this.

He shut the door and locked it.

Unable to stand the lonely cold, he slowly followed Harry's path upstairs. The afternoon sun was giving way to the late winter evening, providing Kit enough light to see by as he made it to the bed. Harry rested on the small bed, in the pool of red and violet light shining through the small window. For the last few nights, they had shared a bed, so Kit knew this wasn't Harry's silent way of dismissing him.

Quietly, Kit stripped off his clothes and tentatively slipped under the covers, pressing his body along Harry's so not to fall off the edge. Harry was awake. Kit could tell by his breathing. He sighed and gently turned, arms enfolding Kit. Kit swallowed, nuzzling in close to Harry's chest, grateful beyond words, wanting to apologize, but unable to speak past the lump lodged in his throat.

Warmth seeped into his skin, making him shiver. He reciprocated Harry's hold and Harry let out an exhausted sigh. "What am I going to do with you?" he asked. It wasn't condescending, it was a genuine question, but not one Kit could give an answer to.

Instead, Kit breathed him in, pressing soft kisses to Harry's collarbone, his furry chest tickling Kit's lips.

Harry released a low sigh as Kit ducked his head to suck a nipple into his mouth. "Kit."

Hearing the hint of protest in Harry's voice, Kit nuzzled Harry's chest and murmured, "I'm cold."

Harry didn't hesitate. He pressed closer. If Harry had any reservations Kit ignored them, instead focusing on the hard press of Harry's cock rubbing against his own.

"Please, Harry," Kit whispered against his ear. "I just want to feel warm. I want to feel you." He didn't think he could take it if Harry rejected him now.

Harry stroked his hand over Kit's cheek and jaw, his gaze locked on Kit's, searching. Kit's breathing quickened. He worked his hand between their flush bodies, squeezing the thick length inside Harry's trousers. Kit tugged at Harry's clothes, desperate to get him naked, to press into the heat of his body. He found Harry's lips, crushing them under his mouth.

"Hey." Harry pulled back enough to speak. "Calm down. What's the rush?"

Kit was shaking. He cleared his throat. "I'm not a very patient man. Let me get a good look at you." Harry obligingly lay back on the pillow, hands lazily caressing Kit's arms and chest. Kit took in the sight before him, naked flesh reflecting the purple and indigo of the waning sunset, his breath catching as Harry's sculpted chest and stomach heaved.

Helping Kit's efforts to undress him, Harry arched up so Kit could strip him of his trousers. Harry had been a marvel to watch from afar, his entire body an exquisite framework of tight, angular muscles and sharp edges, flexing and bunching under his skin as he moved. But up close he was a work of art. Every part of him was honed to perfection, the dark hair coating his skin emphasizing the musculature, gathering in the contours of his arms, chest and stomach, leading down a thick trail of fur to his long cock, which jutted proudly from the dark thatch, reaching for Kit and spilling a single, glistening tear. His withered arm, pale and naked, lent him a vulnerability like a fallen god. Kit stroked the pattern of scars. Harry tensed beneath his touch.

"I need you inside me." It was a plea, his voice shaking.

Harry tensed again. "I... I have never..."

"Never?"

"I've had sex. But with...others, I was always the receiver," he finished with a nervous laugh. It broke some of the remaining tension between them.

"Well, I'm not particular. If you prefer, I'd gladly ride you whichever way."

Harry shook his head, his nose brushing Kit's, and said, "You don't have to pretend with me, Kit."

Kit stared up at him, heart thudding a violent beat in his chest. *I'm not pretending*, he wanted to protest, but instead as he looked into Harry's soft amber eyes found himself saying, "It's...difficult for me. But, with you, I want to be honest, as much as I can be."

"That's all I ask." Harry met his gaze and kissed his forehead.

Kit swallowed. "I want you, however I can get you."

The faint trace of a mischievous smile quirked his lips. "Then, if you'll permit me." With strong but gentle hands, Harry flipped their positions, pressed Kit into the mattress and parted his legs. Nestled comfortably between them, cock to cock, he said, "I'd like to fuck you."

Kit's chest swelled, his heart flipping and his cock flexing under Harry's weight. "I'm in your care, Dr. Woodsman."

Harry laughed, breathy and filthy, relieving the tightness in Kit's stomach. He leaned in, taking possession of Kit's mouth. Kit surrendered completely, wrapping his arms and legs around Harry, pushing their bodies as close as possible.

At this angle, Harry's cock nudged insistently at Kit's entrance. Kit welcomed it, angling his hips, relishing the delicious press and slight burn against his sensitive skin. "Harry," Kit pleaded.

Harry pulled away, panting. "Not yet."

Kit felt the effort it took for Harry to back off. As before, Harry performed his delightful, tormenting descent down his body, and once more Kit was singing his pleasure, his entire body alive with every heated touch of Harry's talented tongue.

Harry eased the tightness clogging Kit's chest, his hands stroking the length of Kit's thighs, firm and kneading. As Kit relaxed into that soothing touch, he gasped when Harry pulled his legs up, bending him in half, spreading his ass, exposing his entrance to Harry and the cool air.

Kit moaned and wiggled in Harry's grip, his opening fluttering in anticipation under Harry's scrutiny. Harry chuckled, staring at him through his spread legs. "I've always wanted to try this."

"Wha —" Kit gave a strangled cry as Harry's tongue flicked over his entrance. Harry's grip on his legs were the only reason he didn't kick out against the new and deeply intimate sensation. The ticklish touch had him jerking in Harry's grip with every swipe of his tongue over his convulsing muscle, begging for more, but not sure what more meant.

"My God!" His hands fisted around the bed sheets as though he would float off the mattress any moment.

Wet heat spread him farther — Harry's tongue diving into him. He was tense and boneless at the same time, helpless against the slippery wet fucking Harry's tongue was giving him. Lips kissing, bristling beard cushioning Kit's spread cheeks, it was so strange, so compelling. His cock dripped a thick line of moisture on his belly, spilling up his chest.

"Harry!"

His pleas were rewarded with the repeated press of Harry's squirming tongue, fucking him softly but thoroughly, tasting as far as it could reach, the pointed tip tickling and teasing his insides until he was a quivering, jabbering mess. He was losing his mind, shattering completely as Harry gently pressed a finger inside, twisting alongside his tongue, the two shapes creating exquisite friction, stretching him until Harry added another finger, sinking in deep as he lapped at Kit's entrance.

"Enough," he gasped. "Please, Harry. Fuck me."

Harry didn't stop, his fingers working in and out, twisting and pressing, searching for Kit's prostate, his mouth never ceasing in kissing and sucking the soft flesh around his asshole. Kit bit his lip, fists beating the mattress, legs trembling as Harry sank deeper. He lost all coherency, mumbling and moaning and panting, trying to communicate how much he needed Harry inside him, needed to feel him more, but unwilling to stop this delicious new realm of pleasure he'd never known existed.

When Harry finally relented, Kit was a trembling mess, stroking Harry thighs, his shoulders, his back, any piece of hot flesh he could reach, anchoring Kit to the earth. Harry released him, allowing him to unbend enough to line up his cock to Kit's wet entrance. He gathered the moisture from Kit's leaking cock and slathered it up and down his cock, the sight so filthy Kit bit his lip to stop a whimper. He was so ready, so desperate. He squirmed and bucked his hips, pressing against Harry's blunt cockhead.

Harry, gentle as ever, took his time, his face flushed. "Kit," he pleaded.

"Yes. Now, Harry," Kit begged.

Gripping Kit's waist, Harry grunted as he pushed his cock inside. Kit hissed and forced his muscles to comply, welcoming Harry's throbbing girth into his body. Inch by inch, Harry sank deeper, slowly and carefully. At one point Kit thought he was full, but Harry kept on going, kept on plundering deeper and deeper until Kit thought he could feel him buried up to his stomach. He swore and panted, never having felt so utterly ravished, so utterly possessed. It was not only Harry's size, which was considerable. A deep warmth was growing inside him, spreading out and filling his chest, his lungs, breathing into the air around them, tingling through his limbs and fingertips. He felt complete, like this was where he was meant to be, at Harry's side, in his arms.

It was terrifying feeling so much at once, but once Harry was fully seated inside Kit's body, Harry shuddered, body held perfectly still, his eyes wet, his mouth open in awe. Kit stroked his arms, murmuring soft encouragements and incoherent praise. Harry was so beautiful, so open and vulnerable in that moment, Kit felt himself falling off a great precipice, but was unafraid of what lay beneath. Harry moved, the smallest grind of his hips. Kit's jaw snapped open, a mindless cry echoing through the sparse room. Harry's length shifted inside him. It was so hot, so strange, but Kit welcomed it, welcomed the slow burn of friction, the throbbing weight of Harry inside him. He released a long breath and clung to Harry, encouraging him to move.

Harry growled, hot plumes of breath gusting against Kit's skin. His face was angelic, his mouth open in wonder, his eyes glowing. Kit urged him down, stroking the planes of his back, clutching his ass, urging him closer. Harry gasped and slowly, carefully rolled his hips, grinding his divine cock against Kit's insides, the thick length filling him completely, driving Kit close to release. The hard press of his fur-covered, muscular stomach stroked Kit's cock.

Harry was trembling against him, his whole body drawn tight. He quickened the pace, thrusting gently. "Kit, you're so beautiful...perfect. I'm..."

"Keep going. Don't...stop."

Harry drove harder, his sweat-dampened skin slapping against Kit's. Kit took it all, thrusting his hips skyward, taking Harry as deep as possible, his muscles clenching and unclenching. Growling again, Harry began to pound into him, his careful manners lost as his pleasure heightened. It wouldn't last long, and neither of them was very graceful as they ground against each other. It was the feverish rutting of two animals finally coming together after a long, hard winter, desperate for life, for each other. But Kit didn't want it to end. He clung desperately to the edges of his release, but threw his head back as Harry fucked liquid heat into his guts, sending him plunging over the edge. His seed erupted between their stomachs and chests, the great swell of warmth enveloping Kit as shudders wracked his body.

Harry was kissing him again, breathless and messy and utterly charming. Kit pulled Harry's full weight against him. He rolled them so Harry lay alongside him, a sated smile curling on his lips.

He shivered when Harry stroked his hand up and down his heated skin before resting it on his hip, his thumb tracing the edges of the brands. Kit caught his breath and said, "Not very subtle, are they?"

"They're healing well."

"I'll take that as a compliment, coming from a doctor." Harry's concerned gaze locked on his. Kit stroked his furry cheek. "Do not think this mark was unjustified. I earned it."

Harry frowned, but his hands didn't stop, his touch gentle. "How?"

Kit looked into those gentle amber-brown eyes and swallowed. He nuzzled a little closer, unable to hold Harry's gaze.

"If it's too painful—"

"No. It's just…" He didn't want Harry to look at him differently. If he knew the truth, if he knew what Kit had done…

"Kit?"

Frantic banging at the door had Kit sitting bolt upright in the small bed, dislodging Harry's arms from around his waist. Harry soon followed, pressing a calming hand to Kit's heaving chest.

"They're here for me."

"Just stay here. I'll see who it is."

Kit gripped Harry's arm, stopping him from leaving the bed.

"Kit, let go."

Kit fought back the compulsion to comply, but found his grip loosening. Harry left the bed, pulling on his trousers and shrugging into his shirt. Kit did the same, grabbing one of Harry's shirts, barely breathing as he watched Harry reach under the bed for his rifle before descending the stairs.

"Harry! Harry!" a frantic woman shouted.

The bolt slid and the door was opened. Kit went to the head of the stairs, crouching awkwardly to peek down. Harry stood in the doorway. A young woman was wrapped around him, clinging fiercely.

"Celeste, what's wrong?"

"It's Father. He needs your help."

Harry pulled back to look at her. "Is the fever back?"

The woman broke out in furious sobs. Her fingers gripped Harry's shirtfront. "No. He was attacked. He won't wake up. Will you come? I've brought you a horse. Please."

Harry didn't hesitate. "Let me get dressed."

He pushed past Kit on the stairs in the near darkness, almost knocking him on his ass. Harry searched the room, picking his clothes free from Kit's.

"I need to go back to Paix. I don't know when I'll be back. There's enough food to last you a few weeks, but I won't be gone that long."

A dark, sinking feeling settled over Kit. Old fears snuck up on him. Harry was going to leave him. He was going to disappear with that woman.

When Harry finished shrugging into his clothes, he banged down the stairs. Kit suppressed his wince as he followed Harry down. The woman saw him, her teary eyes wide with obvious shock at the sight of Kit, or more likely his state of undress—he was wearing one of Harry's shirts and only the shirt. Kit played it up, leaning against the wall and crossing his arms, the oversized shirt sliding off one shoulder. With a lecherous smile curling on his lips, he drawled, "Good evening, my dear."

She gaped. Harry heard and turned, surprised to find Kit and his display. He quickly recovered and went to Kit at the bottom of the stairs.

Kit regarded him from under heavy lids. "Will you be long?" He reached out and straightened Harry's collar, aware of the woman's eyes on them.

Harry threw a concerned glance at the woman before stroking Kit's cheek, his touch warm despite the cold pouring in through the open door, his brow furrowed. Kit pressed into his touch, lips brushing Harry's palm.

"I'll be back as soon as I can." His fingers traced Kit's scratchy stubble. He hesitated before adding, "Don't go anywhere."

Kit offered him a languid smile, ignoring the churning in his gut. "Don't worry about me. It sounds like you're needed, Dr. Woodsman."

Harry's eyes remained concerned. Kit drew him in and kissed him with a passion he didn't feel and had Harry pushing away from him, concern and confusion marring his brow. "What's wrong?"

Kit forced a lascivious smile, stroking his hand down Harry's shirt where the woman had wrinkled the fabric. "Nothing. Go. Hurry back."

Harry didn't look convinced, but he nodded and moved off, shrugging into his coat. "Bolt the door after me."

Kit eyed the woman over Harry's shoulder, daring her to comment. Her eyes had narrowed, as though she was unsure what to make of Kit. He kept his smile painfully in place.

"Got everything?" Harry asked.

Kit jolted, wondering what he was talking about, then realized he was addressing the woman.

"I think so," she answered, teary eyes flickering from Kit to Harry. She held Harry's bag in her hands.

Harry turned back to Kit. "You sure you'll be all right?"

Some of Kit's malice deflated at Harry's persistence. Kit could only nod.

They left, leaving a chilly draught in their wake. Kit bolted the door as he'd been instructed, left alone in the silence. Even the constant creaking and croaking of the wooden structure seemed to have stopped, as though all the life had left with Harry.

She, the woman, had known where to find Harry's bag. She'd been here before. Alone with Harry?

Under his old master he'd have made an enemy of her. A single lingering glance in the wrong way at his master and she would have lost her situation. And Kit would have done it all without a flicker of pity.

That old urge niggled at his mind and his jaw clenched. But he had no power to accomplish it and Harry, unlike his old master, would not delight in his display of vicious, possessive jealousy.

Harry would hate him.

The door caught his attention, the need to leave pressing in on him once more.

It would happen eventually. His true nature was so close to the surface, its ugliness already affecting how Harry looked at him. What would he do if he knew what Kit was?

Kit pressed his hand to the door, the other still on the bolt. He began to shake. Clenching his fist, he let loose a growl before banging it against the wood, making the bolt rattle. He couldn't leave. Harry had told him to stay, wanted him to stay.

He was cold. He wanted to get back in Harry's bed, preferably in Harry's arms.

Magic infused the air, choking Kit's senses.

Sucking in a sharp breath, he turned.

Pressure closed over his mouth, a hand smothering his shocked cry. He clawed and scratched at the arm restraining him, tried but couldn't bite the gloved fingers. He opened his senses, drawing on any magic his attacker possessed. The edges of Kit's vision darkened.

"Easy, Leonor. Sleep. It's time to go home."

Chapter Eight

Somewhere under the blood and meat, the bruises and lacerations, Francis lay fighting for his life. It took over an hour for Harry to treat the worst of his wounds. Twice he had stopped breathing. Harry had fought furiously to keep him going, with Celeste at his side, assisting where she could.

He sat at Francis' bedside, watching the old man's chest rise and fall. He had washed his hands, but blood persisted under his fingernails. His scarred arm trembled. He clenched his fist until it stopped.

The chair opposite him creaked. Celeste reached over and rubbed Harry's shoulder. She had a strong grip. Working hard rearing her brothers and caring for her father in her mother's place all these years had aged her, but also made her strong, resilient. Harry forcibly relaxed his hand and looked into her stern face, her tears were long gone. She had a smear of her father's blood on her chin.

"Who did this to him?" Harry asked.

"The Blue Crows. They arrived in Paix last night, demanding rooms for a small army. Don't know what they want around here. Hasn't been a witch in these parts since before the war." Her voice matched her sturdy grip.

Looking down at the old man's battered face, Harry's voice dropped to a growl. "Why did they attack Francis?"

"Dad was stabling the carthorse when the Crows dragged Joe Tillow from the tavern and started roughing him up. Dad got involved, shouting for them to stop. They warned him to stay away. I tried to get him back in the house. By the time the boys arrived they were beating him." She cleared the tremble from her voice. "I should have done something."

Harry gripped her fingers. "You did the right thing. You know what they'd have done to you." Arresting her would have been the least of it. Harry didn't want to imagine what else they would have done.

"At least I'd know I tried."

"And what would have happened to the boys then? They wouldn't survive a day without you."

At that she stifled a bitter laugh. "True." She put her hand on top of his. "Thank you for this, Harry."

Guilt punched him in the throat. The Crows were here because of Harry, because he was hiding Kit. "I should go and find a place to stay tonight."

Celeste pressed a little closer. Harry could count the small smattering of freckles on her nose and cheeks. "You could stay here. There's not much room." Her tentative fingers stroked the back of his hand. "But I don't mind sharing."

Harry pulled away as gently as he could. "Celeste, I don't—"

"Sorry. Not the best time. I know. Just feeling a little fragile right now, thought I'd test the water. But I think I've already lost my chance."

"I'm sorry."

Celeste waved off his apology and said, "Don't be silly. I was just surprised. So, who is he?"

"What?"

"Dad said you had someone staying with you, someone special. I admit I was a little surprised when I saw him like that—" She cut off her words, her cheeks blushing.

"Did Francis tell anyone else? About Kit? Did he tell the Crows?"

"No. I mean, I don't know why he would. Why?"

"Did you?"

"No. I wouldn't. Why? What's wrong?"

"I need to go."

"Harry?"

"I'll leave a tincture to help prevent infection and some powders for the pain. You'll need to get more bandages."

"Harry, what's going on?" She grabbed for his arm. He evaded her, packing away his bag.

"Take care of your father."

With that he was out of the house and running to the stables.

A pair of Crows turned the corner just as Harry reached the stable doors. He staggered to a halt, ducking into the nearest open stall. Its tethered occupant gave a disgruntled snort before returning to his hay net.

Harry held his breath. Footsteps grew closer. He cursed himself for not having a weapon, having left his rifle behind at the cabin. Slowly, he opened his bag and rifled through its contents, wincing when the metal tools jingled and clattered against one another under his fingers. Closing his fingers around a scalpel, he listened as the Crows' mumbled conversation grew sharper the closer they got. Drawing the small blade free, he waited, breath held.

Harry jumped when a gruff voice shouted somewhere from behind.

"We're moving out. You've got five minutes to get your shit together."

The Crows cursed and murmured something about only just getting settled in. Their footsteps shrank away, retreating from the stables.

Harry slumped back into the bed of straw, his heart wedged somewhere in his throat.

With the little coin he possessed, he paid for a horse and rode out of the village. He kept a steady pace until he was out in the open fields then urged the horse into a full-fledged gallop. All the while he kept his eyes peeled for any sign of the Crows, but the road was blessedly free of their presence.

Riding his horse hard, Harry reached his land in record time. His mount gave a disapproving grunt when he dismounted clumsily. Having not performed such a move in many years, and never having been very skillful at it, Harry went down hard, stumbling into a roll, landing on his shoulder and hip awkwardly until regaining his feet. He cursed and hobbled to the house. He could barely make it out in the darkness. No fires had been lit. Ignoring the dread tightening his throat, Harry went to the front door. Holding his breath, he pressed his hand to the door.

The creak of wood. The rumble of voices.

Harry backed up.

"Aren't you going in?"

Harry stiffened, his fist clenching at Tariq's voice. Turning, he was greeted with a grim smile. This time Tariq was sure, there was no questioning it. The gleam of recognition blazed in his eyes.

The door burst open behind him. Soldiers adorned with blue avian insignias filed out from inside, weapons drawn and aimed at Harry.

Turning his grimace from Harry, Tariq nodded to his men. A kick to the back of Harry's calf sent him to his knees. Harry gritted his teeth, grunting as he hit the floor.

"Last time we were here," Tariq said, leaning in close, staring down at Harry with disgust, "something about you bothered me." He fastened his grip on Harry's scarred arm, his fingers biting into tight muscle. Harry hissed through his teeth. Tariq held up Harry's mottled hand. "How did this happen?"

"The war," Harry bit out.

"Funny, it was my understanding no one survived the Madness of Rasacara."

Harry's heart stopped. He met Tariq's smug glare, giving away nothing.

A soldier came into view. "I have it, sir." He brandished and handed over Harry's rifle. Tariq took it, smiling. "You thought I didn't notice." He ran his hand up the gun's length in admiration. "This insignia. You've done well to try and remove it. It belonged to the lost Western Infantry regiment, the regiment obliterated on that forsaken island. How did you come by such a weapon, I wonder?" With a nod to his men he ordered, "Strip him."

Harry struggled and fought. He'd managed to get to his feet when a punch to his kidney and an iron grip on his throat sent him back to his knees. Another hit to his stomach had him doubling over and hacking up bile. Two Crows moved in to restrain his arms as a blade sliced through his shirt. Tariq removed his leather gauntlet and knelt. His rough hand gripped Harry's wrist, his fingers pressing against the patchwork of scars. He worked his way along Harry's arm. Finding nothing, he moved back up, his grip tightening as he went, his teeth bared. Frustrated, Tariq dug his nails into Harry's skin, reaching past Harry's elbow.

Harry forced himself to keep breathing.

Tariq smiled. Just shy of Harry's armpit, his fingers rubbed over the contorted set of brands distorted within the burn scars.

Every muscle down Harry's back locked. Cold sweat chilled his skin and his heart thumped so hard in his temples he thought he might faint. He kept his gaze focused on Tariq's.

"I thought I knew you. Not your face, but these." He bit his fingers into Harry's biceps. "These have my name written all over them." He sniffed at the flesh as though he could smell the residue of his magic on Harry. "Take a good look, lads. This is the man who single-handily destroyed the armies of Rasacara and Rashivim."

Hushed murmurs sounded from the men, hissed, uneasy words that sounded like "the Madness".

Tariq was still looking at Harry when he ordered, "Take him."

They fitted Harry with heavy irons, the cuffs around his wrists connecting to a matching pair on his ankles with a length of chains just long enough for him to stand straight.

Harry didn't fight. A shroud of guilt weighed him down more effectively than any restraints. He'd evaded justice for so long, tried so long to atone for the past. He closed his eyes and saw baby Henrietta and felt the tiny weight of Davy Junior in his hands. It wasn't enough. It would never be enough.

He daren't look around the small life he had created, to see the uneaten meals and unread books, the unfinished work, scared it would pull him apart, terrified he might break down and scream for Tariq to kill him now and be done with it.

They threw him inside the house, filing in behind him. Some took up position at the door, others at the window.

The rhythmic clanging of metal chains sent sharp spikes of anxiety through Harry, his skin alive with gooseflesh and his last meal wedged at the back of his throat. He shivered, his mind bent on what horrors awaited him. He tried to stand. A sharp tug on the chain and Harry lurched forward. Losing his footing, he went down hard onto wooden boards. A face he didn't know glared down at him.

"I lost good friends in Rasacara, good men you butchered. This is for them."

A swift kick to Harry's stomach had him curling in a tight ball, wheezing and vomiting up what little he had in his stomach. Another kick followed. Bile spewed from his lips. Blows rained down on his back and legs. More Crows moved in to get a piece of him. He brought up his hands to protect his head, leaving the rest of his body vulnerable. Pain ripped through his chest. His vision blurred. Every part of him was cold and broken.

"That's enough. I need him alive."

He was pulled roughly to his feet, screaming airlessly against the agony ripping him apart from the inside out. Coppery blood filled his mouth. He coughed before it choked him. It sprayed over the azure crow adorning the nearest soldier's tunic. The fist that struck him snapped his head back, splitting open his lip, blood flooding his nose. It was only the other Crow's grip on his arms keeping him from collapsing to the ground. He closed his eyes. His chest heaved, every breath shooting white-hot bolts of agony through his abdomen.

His world fell into absolute darkness. They were binding his eyes. A coarse cloth was wedged into his mouth and tied tight, forcing him to make a grim, stretched smile.

"General, what about his magic?"

Tariq chuckled. "He's branded. If he could use his power, don't think for a moment we wouldn't all be dead by now. He's harmless." Harry flinched when a hand slapped his cheek playfully. "But I've a use for him."

"But, sir, if he is the Madness of Rasacara, Emperor Aralias granted him exoneration —"

A sharp silence fell over the house.

When Tariq spoke, his words were soft, dangerous. "Do not utter that man's name in my presence."

"Yes, General," the Crow sputtered. "Forgive me."

The hit, when it came, knuckles crunching against bone, threw Harry back on his ass. Pain blossomed over his cheek, throbbing through his jaw. Wet heat erupted over his chin — blood pumping from his split lip. A boot was pressed to the back of his neck, forcing his face into the mud. He gasped and choked.

"He deserves death, but not yet."

The boot was removed. Harry gagged. He rolled onto his side so the blood collecting in his mouth didn't choke him. It soaked into the gag.

Cold darkness tickled the inside of Harry's skin — his magic, pulsing so close to the surface. Bile gurgled up his throat. The scent and taste of blood. The crazed eyes of the dead and dying. Madness eating at men's minds. He retched, pushing the darkness back, holding on tight with slippery fingers.

"We should send for Jack and Hal." Harry picked out the words through the throbbing in his temples and the crackle in his breathing.

"No," Tariq said. "He'll be here soon."

"Sir?"

Tariq didn't answer.

Another grave silence fell over the house.

Weak and disorientated, Harry struggled to piece together what they wanted, what Tariq was planning.

Kit. They wanted Kit.

Where was he? Why wasn't he here? He'd promised he'd wait. But he'd gone.

If he was gone it meant he was safe.

Harry closed his eyes behind the blindfold, his mind plunging into welcoming darkness.

He wished they'd had the chance for a real farewell.

* * * *

The world was spinning, or maybe it was Kit. No, his cheek was firmly planted against the dewy blades of grass tickling his nose and lips. His head was too heavy to lift. He blinked and realized it was his eyes spinning, unable to focus. The flickering torchlight and soft mumble of strange voices didn't help. A blue bird fluttered at the center of his swirling vision.

Scrunching his eyes shut, Kit clung to the scraps of recent memory filtering through his foggy mind. He'd been warm, lying on a too-firm mattress with an even firmer, much more pleasant Harry. But something had taken away that rare moment of peace. A woman, draped and crying over Harry. Harry leaving him. Kit remembered rage, jealousy and…fear.

The Blue Crows had found him.

Kit tensed his muscles, trying to move. His arms were bound behind his back. His mind and stomach protested the smallest shift. He tried opening his eyes again. The world was still tilting. His mouth was dry and aching. Trying to wet his lips, his tongue caught on the wet cloth cutting into his lips and cheeks.

The blue bird he saw came into focus, sharpening into the insignia on the back of the Crow's uniform. There were two of them. Both stood with their backs to Kit, guarding him. They were talking, but Kit couldn't make out their murmured words.

Kit took stock of the pain around his body. His chest was tight. Pins and needles tingled through his right arm where he lay on it. The cold had his branded hip throbbing angrily as he tried to move.

The recently familiar scents and sights of woodland were bizarrely reassuring. They couldn't have taken him far from Harry's cabin. Why? Why had they brought him here? Where were the rest of the Crows?

Scrabbling together the weak, addled specks of his adrenaline, Kit felt a cold thread of heady magic assault his senses. It was dark and difficult to translate, but Kit knew it instantly.

Harry.

With great effort, Kit summoned all his will into pushing Harry's dark magic aside, seeking out the less complex power mingling in the air. Breathing in deeply, he caught a whiff off one of his guards.

It was new, not something he'd tried to harness before, but he'd felt it, just before the world had gone black inside the shack. Closing his eyes, he let it fill him, then manipulated it to his will. After the touch of Harry's magic, it was easy to pull at the threads of this simple power. With a grunt, he figured it out, untangling the threads and fusing them to his soul, attracting the guard's attention.

One turned, astonishment marring his shadowed face.

Kit concentrated on the syphoned magic and blinked out of existence, only to reappear a second later, lying in the same heap a few feet away. It was enough to give him an advantage as the Crows scoured the darkness before one of them spotted him and shouted to the other.

Kit focused the magic on his bonds, not even sure if it would work. He phased out again, just for a split second, reappearing in the same spot, leaving his bonds behind in an empty tangle. Arms and legs protesting as blood rushed back into his tingling limbs, Kit grunted around the gag. He struggled to his feet and pulled the gag free, working his aching jaw.

He ran, welcoming the small, cold pulses of Harry's magic guiding him through the forest. His hip protested, but he pushed through the pain.

A Crow appeared before him out of thin air and pushed him back, sending him sprawling and landing painfully in an ungainly heap. He tried to roll with the force and regain his feet, but the air had been knocked from his lungs on impact, leaving him heaving for breath.

"Jack!" the other Crow shouted to the one leering over Kit with a grim smile. "He still has magic. We need to warn Tariq."

"Go. I'll keep him here."

The other Crow lingered, hesitating.

"Go!"

He went, fleeing through the trees.

"Stay down."

Kit moved to disobey, coughing. In a flash he was pushed down again, groaning as his back hit the wet earth.

"I said *stay*."

Kit grimaced. He rolled onto all fours. A sharp kick met his stomach. He fell to his side, choking on bile, chest heaving.

A hand gripped his hair, yanking his head up. "Why is it everyone fears you, Leonor?" he whispered close to Kit's ear. "I expected so much more." Releasing his grip, the Crow disappeared. Kit's face fell into the dirt. When the Crow spoke again, his voice was distant. "So many stories about you, the great magic you wielded, and the scores of men you killed. A great warrior, favorite of the Witch Army general himself. I don't see it personally. Why don't you show me?"

Kit spat acid into the grass and heaved himself up, arms shaking. The Crow's booted foot hit his back, stomping him into the ground.

"Come on." Stomp. "Show me." Stomp. "*Show me!*"

Kit coughed, tasting blood.

"Ha! I knew it. Nothing but Tariq's salivating little bitch."

Lying limp in the dirt, chest heaving, Kit began to laugh.

The Crow pressed down on his spine. "What's this? Lost your mind?"

He coughed again. "I was so much more than that."

The Crow chuffed and raised his boot again. Kit drew the magic in, feeling it claw under his skin. It fused with his body, his blood and bones, translating until he understood its unique tongue. Kit phased and reappeared less than a second later behind the Crow. The Crow spun, fist raised. Kit got in first with a back-handed slap, shocking the Crow more than anything. His head snapped back to Kit, face red with rage and humiliation. Kit felt the change in pressure as the Crow set to phase again. Kit gripped his arm. The Crow snarled and tried to shake him off. Kit caught his other wrist, fingernails digging in.

They blinked out of existence and back, Kit keeping them in place, their forms flickering. The Crow gaped in shock, then glared and snarled, kicking out at Kit's legs. Kit grunted, baring his teeth. His grip slipped and the Crow went for his sword. Before he could pull it free from its sheath, Kit pressed the palm of his hand to the Crow's chest. The Crow tried to phase again. Kit held him in place and pushed his hand forward. The Crow gasped, flickering, staring down at where Kit's fist disappeared inside his chest, phasing through flesh and bone. He choked, wide eyes meeting Kit's.

Kit smiled and leaned forward, hissing into his ear as his fist tightened around the Crow's frantic heart, "I was his weapon."

The Crow gaped, mouth working silently, nothing but breathless gags escaping his petrified stupor.

With a sneer, Kit tightened his grip around the failing muscle, each slowing beat draining a little more light from the Crow's eyes. Blue, Kit noted. *Tariq always liked blue eyes.* He ripped his fist free, feeling every stretch and snap of arteries, cold air enveloping the hot organ, warm blood splattering his arm, arcing up to his neck as he squeezed. Warm drops splashed and quickly chilled on his cheek.

The Crow gave a final rattling grunt before collapsing forward, his magic dissipating to nothing before he hit the ground. Kit took a step back, glaring down at the dead man. At his chest, the breast of his uniform was unmarred, with no evidence of Kit's attack. Kit took in the red pulp that remained of the heart inside his fist.

He let it fall to the grass with an empty thump.

He blinked at the gore, seeing it with new eyes. His body had moved on its own, vicious and swift just like he'd been taught, to take down the enemy before they landed a fatal blow, but making it a spectacle, a show. His master would have been so proud. So fucking proud.

His bloody hand began to shake. Clutching his throat, he gagged until vomit poured forth, sending him to his knees in violent spasms. When nothing more would come up, when the smell of blood was all he could taste, he wept silently.

Nothing had changed. No matter how far he ran, not matter how much time spanned between the weapon he'd been to the broken man he'd survived to become, he was forever his master's monster.

He retched again, but nothing came out.

An icy shadow of magic called to him, waking him with tingling shivers up and down his back. Harry's magic. It was dark and cruel and comforting, drawing him back. It swelled, a cold, heavy darkness infecting him, dangerous and glorious. He let it fill him, breathing it in, and stopped shaking, its invisible power, Harry's far-off presence, giving him strength enough to rise.

Harry was in trouble or hurt. There was no other reason for Kit to feel his magic so strongly from so great a distance.

Weak and dizzy, he ran blindly, following the bolstering darkness, letting it lead him through the trees. He'd taken only a few steps when the thread of magic snapped, a candle snuffed out, leaving Kit gasping for its familiar presence.

A cold breath chilled Kit's chest, leaving him empty and aching. He was lost, but started to run again. Despite the fierce protests of his hip and the tightness of his chest and new aches, he kept his pace steady, reaching, hoping for the consoling touch of darkness inside Harry.

Then a spark of familiar magic joined the dark, tangled web of Harry's. Heat erupted in his blood.

Tariq.

Kit clenched his jaw, the familiar power a clinging embrace which he could not escape. He fought the wave of nausea accompanying it and pushed on through the trees.

He reached the shack. In the darkness the yard was empty and silent, the only sound Kit's heavy breathing and the pounding heartbeat in his skull. Nothing moved. The forest was silent beyond the usually flittering of wildlife. No men, no horses, but magic lingered in the air. Tariq's magic.

He took a careful, staggering step back, then another. Fire burst behind him. Kit leaped forward, almost crashing to the ground to escape it. Cutting off his retreat, the flames grew before his eyes, expanding left and right, creating a ring around the house and yard, trapping him.

He tasted Tariq's magic, opened himself up to it.

The scars on his hip burned. He fell to his knees, writhing in agony. The magic abandoned him, leaving him cold and shaking.

Through blurry eyes, Kit scanned the house, finding a figure in the open doorway. Smug-faced, with his arms folded, Tariq looked down at him. "Hello, little one."

Heart pounding in his temples, Kit reached blindly for any magic in the air. A dark slither floated out of reach. He knew it was Harry's. He tried to pull it into himself. A blast of burning pain along his brands had him crying out in agony until he couldn't breathe. He released his hold on the magic and the pain ebbed away once more, leaving him gasping on the ground.

"I wouldn't advise trying that again, little one. You should know by now not to test me."

Kit gritted his teeth as Tariq sent another jolt of searing pain through the brand. He grunted, holding back his scream until the connection faded again.

"I take it Jack didn't make it?" Tariq stood over him, gesturing to Kit's crimson hand and bloodied sleeve.

Kit clenched his trembling fist to his chest, his skin tight under the dried gore.

Tariq shook his head. He gave a sad sigh and crouched low, leaning in close to say softly, "I thought my brand didn't take effect. We were too rushed last time, but no matter. Now we've got all the time in the world."

Kit flinched back, glaring at Tariq. "You sent that man to his death. You knew I'd kill him."

"Oh, little one, don't blame me. It's just your nature. You're a born killer. I knew it from the first."

Kit trembled, and he hated himself for it.

"I missed you, little one. Now it's time to come home."

"No," Kit said, his voice shaky. He reached out for magic, desperate. Pain seared his skin until he was blind with tears and he was forced to loosen his grip.

Tariq's eyes narrowed. "Don't be difficult, Chris."

"I won't go with you."

Tariq smiled then sighed again. "I don't have time for this." Tariq whistled, stepping back. Crows emerged from the shack, weapons drawn. "Bind him."

Kit glared and snarled, daring the closest Crows to strike first. They hesitated, looking at one another uncertainly. Kit scrambled to his feet and the Crows flinched.

"Stop that, little one. I may be able to wield flames, but I can be rather clumsy with a blade."

Kit's head snapped to Tariq. At Tariq's feet Harry, beaten and bloody, knelt slumped, half naked and bound in irons. Tariq gripped a fistful of Harry's hair, exposing his throat. In his other hand he held a blade, pressed under Harry's jaw. Harry's eyes were covered, and a soiled gag was wedged in his mouth. Harry's powerful body was awash with grime and blood, his skin mottled with cuts and deep, ugly bruises.

"You fucker!" Kit snarled, readying to attack.

"Don't think about it, little one. I would like the pair, you and this slippery bastard, but if needs be I will settle for one. What will it be?" Harry's blood oozed, shining on the steel blade.

Kit glared at Tariq, hesitating.

Breathing hard through clenched teeth, he sank to the ground and sat back on his heels, muscles bound tight with rage. Accepting his surrender, Tariq nodded to his men. Kit allowed them to bind him with irons matching Harry's, arms tied behind his back.

"Good boy, little one."

"Let him go."

Tariq grinned. "You can't be serious."

"You came here for me. You have me. Harry has nothing to do with this."

Tariq handed Harry off to his men, ignoring Kit now he was securely bound.

"You don't need him. What use is he to you?"

Tariq surprised him with a bark of laughter. "You're losing your touch, little one."

"What are you talking about?"

Tariq laughed again. "Allow me to introduce the two of you properly. Christopher Leonor, former Blue Crow, traitor and deserter, this is Henry Tallis, former military surgeon of the Western Front Infantry and later the famed Madness of Rasacara."

Kit stared past Tariq to Harry, beaten and unconscious, helpless as a spring lamb. "You're wrong."

"Afraid not."

"Don't you think if he possessed such power, he would have used it against you by now?" Kit thought not. Harry feared it his magic. "Don't you think *I* would have used it?"

Tariq's voice grew harsh at that. "You know nothing, little one. I saw Rasacara first-hand when we made it ashore. This monster was the only one left. I branded and bound his magic on the emperor's order. He's harmless now."

Branded? Kit had seen every part of him...

The burns on Harry's arm. They had been Tariq's doing.

Seething with rage on Harry's behalf, Kit clung to a hopeful thought.. Tariq didn't know Harry still had access to his magic.

He had touched it. Kit had felt the raw power swirling inside Harry. The Madness. Harry was the witch who had massacred two armies in a matter of hours. Kit shuddered, recalling the unbridled strength, Harry's pain.

Unceremoniously, Kit was grabbed and pushed deeper into the forest, where horses and carts were hidden among the thick cluster of trees. He didn't fight. He was hauled into a cart. Iron bars secured him and a canvas cover was thrown atop it. He caught a glimpse of Harry being dumped into a similar cage before he disappeared from sight. He looked dead, slumped over on his bloody face, but his chest had heaved with labored breaths.

What he was, whatever he'd done, Kit couldn't fight the need to get to him.

The earth glowed with the smouldering embers of Tariq's fire. Kit breathed in and out, concentrating on the magic. His brands flared hot, stinging his flesh. *Fuck.* It hurt so much, as though acid was being poured into an open wound. Clenching his jaw against the pain, he'd almost given up when he managed to conjure a flame inside the cart.

"Stop him!" Tariq's voice boomed over the yard.

Too late. The canvas caught quickly and, with Kit's encouragement, spread to the wooden base and wheels. Kit gasped in pain before covering his mouth as smoke filled the small space.

"Get him out of there!"

Kit felt Tariq's attempt to quell the flame. He fought back until the pain grew too much then cradled his head on the far side of the cart. The metal bars swung open and Kit was rescued by the Crows. The flames burned out under Tariq's influence, leaving a charred wooden carcass.

Kit was brought before Tariq. His face almost purple with rage, he hissed, "Clever little bitch." He pulled back his fist and punched Kit hard in the stomach. Kit gagged and gasped airlessly, falling limp in the Crows' arms. "Throw him in with Tallis. We're losing time."

Once safely hidden under the canvas, Kit reached for Harry, gingerly nudging his face against Harry's cheek. "Harry," he whispered, voice hoarse from the smoke and the punch to the gut.

A soft raspy groan came from Harry's split lips.

"Harry," he repeated, that simple groan a lifeline for him to cling to, a shining glint of hope. He didn't know what to say. He had no reassurance to offer, was unsure if Harry would even understand him.

Kit nuzzled in close, his nose and lips brushing Harry's. Harry shuddered. *He must be freezing.* Kit shuffled farther up, carefully bending his body to fit close against Harry's — difficult without the use of his arms. Harry winced, lifting his head to rest it against Kit's shoulder. Kit dropped his chin to rest it atop Harry's head, breathing him in, kissing his hair.

Harry croaked beneath him, his body trembling. "Idiot." *Cough.* "Why did you come back?"

Harry's ashen skin was rough with gooseflesh. He'd thought Kit had left. He could have. After killing Jack, he could have turned his back and run. But he hadn't. He'd come back for the same reason he hadn't left sooner — he adored this man, without motive or fear. If it made him a fool, he couldn't bring himself to care in this moment.

"I knew you'd do something stupid like let the Crows beat you and chain you up."

Harry gave something close to a dry choking laugh. Kit soothed him as best he could until Harry's breathing evened out, pressing his lips to Harry's hair, blowing warm plumes of air into his scalp.

"You shouldn't have come back. This was always going to happen."

"What are you talking about?"

It took Harry so long to reply, Kit thought he must have lost consciousness. "I...so many dead... I killed so many. I deserve to die."

Kit's heart constricted. The surrender, the finality of defeat in Harry's voice, tore at him. Gritting his teeth, he huddled closer, clearing his throat before he could speak. "It was war."

Harry tried to shake his head, wincing and groaning, a hideous choking noise tearing from his throat. "No. Not like that. No man, enemy or no, deserves such a horrendous end. Dying in fear." Harry's chest heaved, his voice giving out for a moment. "You shouldn't have come back. You have to escape."

Kit tried again to seek out a scrap of magic. The brand burned his hip and he smothered his whimper so to not worry Harry. "If you deserve to die, what about me? The things I've done... If you're a monster, what does that make me?"

Harry didn't answer. Kit wasn't sure Harry even heard him. The silence was a painful blessing. Harry didn't stir when the cart began to move, rocking on the rough forest terrain.

Chapter Nine

The world was dark and cold and painful. It no longer swayed—a small mercy on Harry's churning stomach. His entire body ached, stiff and tender. He couldn't summon the will to test the condition of his beaten body. Even so, his brain began to categorize his injuries. At least two fractured ribs judging from the radiating pain in his chest with every inhalation, multiple contusions, and he wouldn't be surprised if he'd be pissing blood from the blows to his kidneys. Wetting his lip, wincing as his split lip cracked anew, he tasted blood. The cloth over his eyes assured him he hadn't gone blind and the numbness in his arms was due to them being bound, not from nerve damage.

Other than the sound of men and horses and the far-off crackle of a campfire, a slow heartbeat thumped under his ear. His head cushioned on an expanding surface. His mind reeled back to comprehend his situation.

Kit.

His solid warmth was the only comfort in his dark world. A pained groan tore from his dry throat before he could stop it.

"Harry, it's all right. I'm here."

Harry couldn't bring himself to speak, not after what he had confessed. He tried moving away, leaving the small circle of warmth Kit had made for them. His right side protested the smallest movement. He grunted and moaned, falling hard onto his bound arms. It took enormous effort not to scream. The blindfold absorbed his tears.

"Don't move," Kit scolded gently. "You're in pretty shit shape."

He heard shuffling and huffs of breath as Kit pressed his body close to his. Harry wanted to cling to that heat, but couldn't stand Kit touching him, didn't want to infect him. Gritting his teeth, he fought to move away. He managed to gracelessly turn around, cold biting at his naked skin.

"Harry?"

"Don't." Harry swallowed. "Don't touch me."

Kit was silent. The distance between them was only a few inches in the tight space, but it could have been stretched over miles. No shared heat, no soft breath, no sturdy heartbeat. Kit would have been safe, but he was once more trapped with Harry.

He flinched when Kit's chin rested on his shoulder and his body pressed close. "But I like touching you. Besides, we need to share heat or you'll freeze. I don't want to lose you to something like that."

Harry heaved with the effort of supressing a choked sob. Why was Kit being so gentle? His heat felt good. He wanted to hold Kit's body close one last time.

"Don't die, Harry. I won't let you, even if you think you deserve it. Don't leave me. I plan to live through this and you're coming with me."

"You have no idea what you're saying."

"Maybe not. I'm cold and starving. If Tariq wants to keep us alive, he's going the wrong way about it."

Harry's brow furrowed. "What do you mean?"

Kit scoffed, but it wasn't directed at Harry. "I think they're taking us to the capital, Noibalon."

Horror swelled in the pit of Harry's stomach. "Why?"

Kit was silent for a long moment, then said, "Believe me, I'm less than thrilled myself. I swore I'd never go back."

Harry's gut clenched. It was too dangerous. There would be too many people. If he lost control, if the darkness broke free... He daren't even think about the chaos it would unleash.

"Kit." He gave a shuddering breath. "You have to kill me."

Deafening silence fell between them. Kit's body was rigid, his rapid heartbeat loud in Harry's ears.

"Kit."

Nothing.

"Kit, did you hear me?"

"Shut up."

"I—"

"I said, shut up. Don't you dare ask that of me."

"It's the only way."

"No."

"I don't want... This, whatever it is inside me, can't be unleashed again. I can't control it. Until Rasacara, I didn't even know it existed."

"How's that possible?" Kit asked, his voice tight.

"It first manifested on the battlefield. I never felt anything or showed any sign of being a witch before then."

Kit was silent for a moment then asked, losing the sharp edge to his voice, "What happened?"

Harry swallowed hard. His arms were heavy, as though laden with Louis' cold, bloodied body once more. He grunted before he could speak. "I was searching the battlefield for injured men. I came across soldiers pointing their guns, not at the enemy, but at one of their own, someone I cared for." His voice broke.

"Louis."

Harry grunted, his heart constricting. "They gunned him down."

"Why?"

"He...Louis, he was out of his mind. The war broke him. He'd wake up screaming, attacking phantom enemies. He was so scared of dying. They put him down like a rabid dog." He stopped, unable to carry on. He closed his eyes on his tears before they fell. Kit pressed closer, his touch stopping Harry from falling apart. "Afterward," he continued when he could, "the darkness erupted through me, spreading out, enveloping every man in its path.

"I was found after, when the ships finally made it to shore, and taken to Niobalon and interrogated. Certain I'd be executed, instead I received my brands. Tariq performed the branding, but something happened. As soon as my flesh started to burn, the darkness stirred, causing Tariq to attack."

"Your arm."

Harry was drained and could barely keep his eyes open, his entire body aching with numerous blows. This was the first time he'd spoken of Louis, and it left him weak and shaken, but a little relieved to finally tell someone else about him, as though it wasn't all a dream, as though what he and Louis had shared was worth telling, worth remembering. Kit pressed his face to Harry's shoulder, offering heat and solace.

Harry couldn't bring himself to say any more and they lay in silence. He didn't realize he'd started to nod off in Kit's warmth until Kit suddenly stiffened. "This is perfect."

Harry frowned. "What do you mean?" His stomach sank, foreboding chilling his already cold skin.

"You can use it." When Harry did nothing but pull back from his embrace, scowling, Kit continued, a smile in his voice. "Use the Madness, the darkness, whatever you call it. Unleash it on the Crows."

Harry snarled in pain as he pulled completely free from him. "You haven't listened to a word I said."

"But it makes sense. They don't know you're untethered. Do it. Do it and we're free. The darkness doesn't affect me. We'll be safe."

Harry shook his head, too tired to get angry. "No."

"Why?" A tremble entered Kit's words.

"This power could wipe out entire villages, cities, maybe entire countries. I don't know how far this evil can spread. I couldn't stand it infecting one more person. You have to kill me, please, Kit. You can end this."

"I won't let that happen."

Harry's voice cracked on a frustrated sob. "You have to."

Kit's voice was hard. "I won't let anyone command me again. Not Tariq, and definitely not you."

Harry sighed, his chest heaving. "You are a fool."

"No more than you."

Footsteps drew close. The deafening rustle of canvas being ripped aside after so long a silence made Harry flinch. Firelight penetrated his blindfold.

"Here you are, lovebirds."

Something hard and dry hit Harry's chest.

"Make sure you share nicely."

Kit growled. "How the fuck do they expect us to eat this?"

"What is it?" Harry asked, his empty stomach making its hunger known with a hollow lurch.

"Salt-dried fish."

The scrabbling and rattling of chains sounded. Kit spoke through gritted teeth. "Here, turn back to me."

Harry hesitated.

"Please, Harry."

Kit's pain tore at him and he obliged. It took some effort, and now he'd felt where his beaten body hurt the worst, but he managed.

"Open your mouth," Kit ground out.

Harry hesitated again, about to refuse, when a wafer of hard meat touched his lips. It was pungent and hard, but he chewed and pulled at the fish, slowly tearing and eating his way through, ignoring the pain of his split lip. His lips met Kit's. For a long second, they stayed there, until Kit tore into the last piece. They continued this, Kit feeding him like a hatchling, their mouths touching gently each time. It was exhausting and messy, but every brush of Kit's lips soothed Harry a little. He had no idea if the Crows were watching them, but right now, he couldn't summon the energy to care.

Kit brushed his nose and cheek over Harry's skin, licking clean the mess on his face. Harry felt himself pressing into that tender touch, nuzzling his face close, breathing in Kit's skin.

"No more talk of dying. We're going to survive this."

Harry was silent. He didn't dare douse Kit's misplaced hope. There was only one way to stop this.

* * * *

They traveled by day, setting up camp each night. Kit fed what little was thrown to them once a day to Harry, leaving a small portion for himself. Harry was still weak and sore from his beating, but as Kit had predicted, Tariq wouldn't let him die.

"He needs treatment," Kit had begged that morning, waking after an uneasy, restless night to find Harry hot to the touch despite his lack of clothing. He had developed a fever and Kit had been at an utter loss for what to do. "Please, he'll die."

The Crow guarding them had shrugged off his pleas, sneering and continuing their slow march across country. It wasn't until Kit had struggled to his feet and rammed his body repeatedly against the bars, screaming, demanding to see Tariq, that the Crows obliged him.

"What's all this shouting for, little one?" Tariq asked once summoned, an unpleasant smile on his face.

"If he's going to be any use to you, he needs a doctor."

"I can't do that, little one."

"You have to do something. Please."

Tariq's smile grew more unpleasant. "What would you do to save him, Chris?"

Kit recoiled, hands gripping knuckle-white on the bars. Swallowing before he could answer, he said, "Anything?"

Tariq regarded him. "You truly care for him, don't you?"

"Please…Master."

Tariq arched a brow at him. The moment stretched, his eyes fixed on Kit. Kit didn't dare look away.

"Very well."

Harry was removed from the cart. Kit closed his eyes, unable to look at Harry.

* * * *

"Come on," a Crow said to Kit later that night, opening the cage. "General wants to see you." There was a knowing smirk on his scarred face, curling his lips grotesquely.

Kit's stomach heaved, but he stood tall and walked as gracefully as the irons would allow, not giving the rat-faced Crow a second glance. He was steered through the camp. From the number of small tents, Kit guessed Tariq had about thirty men with him. It was a considerably smaller number compared to the great witch army Tariq had once commanded.

A thought came to him as he took in the men sitting around fire pits, eating, drinking and inspecting weapons, their faces sallow and grim, their uniforms caked with mud and showing signs of wear. Was this it? Was this all that remained of the Blue Crows?

He couldn't help the small, satisfied smirk tugging at the edge of his lips.

He didn't recognize most of them men he shuffled past, though they clearly knew who he was, glaring up at him as they checked over their rifles or picked at their meager rations. He reached out tentatively for magic. There were glimmers, pale and weak. The realization struck Kit to the bone. These men weren't witches. Well, most of them. Most of them were ordinary soldiers.

Arriving at the obviously much larger and grander tent, Kit was stopped and his irons removed. Tariq didn't expect him to fight. He was right. Not with Harry's life in the balance. Back straight, he swallowed and entered.

Tariq sat lazily, his uniform removed and replaced with a dark, fur-trimmed robe. Age was catching up with him, but more than that, the deep creases around his eyes and mouth spoke of stress and hardship. Never a handsome man, his large, powerful presence made up for his rough, stony features. It was his smile, confident and strangely alluring, that had once ensnared Kit, made him do anything to have that approval aimed at him. It didn't look like Tariq had much to smile about these days. Indeed, when he looked Kit up and down, assessing him with a critical eye, his face was rigid and craggy. Kit had no idea how old Tariq was. In the early days, he had seemed eternal and unmoving to Kit. Not anymore. Now he was old and tired.

His voice was deeper too, gruff and aged as the rest of him. "Come."

Kit went to him. He stopped just out of arm's reach. "Closer."

Kit moved, looking down at his former master, fighting to hide his contempt. Tariq put his hand up when Kit was less than a handful of inches from him. He scowled and stood. Kit refused to step back, despite

Tariq's proximity, despite his robe brushing Kit's shirt front, his breath warm on Kit's skin. It disturbed and delighted Kit to discover he had to look down at his former master. He stood a good three inches taller, unsettling his equilibrium formed from years of having to look up to meet his master's gaze.

He smelled the same, a perfume of jasmine and exotic spices costing more than his armor and weapons, struggling to hide the musk of sweat and horses after days riding. Kit didn't smell too fresh himself.

Tariq took hold of Kit's jaw, turning him to look at his profile. Kit allowed it, jaw clenched, hands flinching into fists.

"You've grown." He rubbed his thumb over Kit's new beard. "When did you last shave?"

"I don't know."

Tariq sniffed disapprovingly, swiping his fingers from Kit's face. Turning away, he walked to the mountain of furs atop a pallet that served as his bed. He sat lazily on the edge, his legs spread, looking Kit up and down again, brow furrowed.

"How long has it been?"

Kit released a steady breath before he could answer, unsure what Tariq was referring to. He settled on, "Ten years since I left the Crows."

"Since you betrayed me and your brothers. Ten years you evaded capture. I'm almost impressed. But you got sloppy, comfortable and ended up putting your trust in the wrong person. I didn't get a good look at you that night when you fled from Lady Bordeaux's home. You've changed."

Kit offered a grim smile. "Growing up will do that."

The scowl deepened on Tariq's face. "So I see. Strip. I want to see you."

Kit hesitated, muscles tensing along his spine. His heart vibrated up his throat, making him dizzy. He opened his mouth to refuse.

"You did say *anything*, little one."

Kit's heart thudded an uneven rhythm. His hands shook. He wanted to vomit. He managed a smile and said, "It seems you've changed too, Master." He pulled at the lace of Harry's borrowed shirt, his heart constricting as Harry's woody sent caught Kit off guard. He let the shirt slip free and flutter to the ground with a mocking flourish.

"Hurry up." The scowl was back on Tariq's face.

Controlling his trembling fingers, Kit managed to unbutton the fly of his trousers. Stepping out of each leg, he threw the trousers aside and he stood before Tariq, naked and waiting.

When Tariq reached out for him again, Kit hesitated before moving into his reach. His breath caught. The gold on Tariq's fingers was cold as it caressed Kit's chest and stomach. Tariq's fingers stroked lower, trailing along the line of golden hair growing from navel to pubis.

"This is new." Tariq tugged at the hair above Kit's cock, grimacing, those new lines around his eyes deepening into great crevices.

Kit swallowed, close to gagging.

Ignoring Kit's cock, Tariq ran his palm over Kit's thigh, fingers playing with the hair, drawing the shape of each muscle. Kit shuddered, fighting back revulsion. "You *have* changed." Back up, Tariq's fingers traced first the witch brand, the one he'd placed there when he had taken Kit from the prison in Rasacara. His hand trailed higher, his fingernails catching on the newly healed, tender flesh of the disfigured tethering brand.

Tariq gave a dark chuckle. "What a mess. I'd have liked to have taken my time with you." His voice was almost tender, close to nostalgic.

Kit recalled that night, the night the Crows had finally caught up to him. He had killed the men Tariq had sent ahead to capture him and had been running blindly to get away when a bolt of red-hot pain had seared into his skin. The attack had been from a distance, but Tariq had always had good aim. But it hadn't been enough. The brand didn't work.

"Do the rest of the men know I have access to magic?"

"It doesn't matter. While you remain close to me, I control you."

"I could still kill a good number of them without magic."

Tariq harrumphed. "But you won't. You're going to behave, aren't you, Chris?"

Tariq released him without waiting for an answer. He picked up a goblet from a table. Wine, always the same expensive vintage from wineries in the empire's southern isles. Kit could almost taste it. Tariq took a healthy swallow. "Kneel."

Kit clenched his jaw and fell to his knees, his eyes locked on Tariq's. He refused to lower his gaze as he'd been taught.

Tariq smiled then laughed aloud. "Don't look at me like that, little one. You used to enjoy this. I remember how you used to beg to sit at my feet."

Kit flinched. Tariq leaned forward, so close Kit thought he was going to kiss him. Kit closed his eyes, clenched his teeth tight against the acid climbing up his throat. Tariq's fingers clamped around his jaw, forcing his head up, the heat of his breath on Kit's skin.

"Do you really think I could bring myself to fuck you, looking like that?"

Kit summoned a sardonic smile from the swell of burning rage and humiliation pulsing in his gut. "What's the matter, Master? Can't stomach fucking someone with a bigger cock than you?" Pulling out of Tariq's hold, he rose to his feet, wiping his mouth even though Tariq's lips hadn't touched his.

Tariq didn't move, gazing up at Kit, managing to look both disgusted and amused.

Kit gathered up his clothes. Slowly and steadily, taking his time to fasten his trousers, he left his shirt open, revealing the body that so offended Tariq. Kit cast his eyes around the tent for the first time, taking it in. It was sparse, no doubt more luxurious and comfortable than the rest of the troops' with his bed of furs, ambient lighting from numerous lanterns and a table topped with wine and meat. But there were stitched patches in the canvas, and the floor was bare where there would have once been rugs strewn about to keep out some of the cold. The furs were matted with visible bald patches, the lanterns mismatched, the meat the same served to Kit and Harry, the wine...

Kit walked to the table, Tariq's eyes following him, and very deliberately poured himself a healthy measure. He held it under his nose before taking a sip. He cringed at the vinegary taste. "Not up to your usual standard." He poured the rest into the grassy earth then picked at the cold meats on a platter, folding slices into his mouth without tasting them. "Who are those men out there? They are not Crows, not matter how you dress them up."

"They are loyal, men who serve me despite your little subterfuge to ruin me." Though he spoke casually, rage smoldered under the surface, tightly contained.

Kit chuffed and said almost sweetly, "Desperate enough to serve even under a disgraced, boy-fucking deviant. What a merry band you lead."

The muscles in Tariq's jaw twitched as though he were chewing a wasp. "Don't provoke me, little one."

Kit smiled. "Why not? This is what you've wanted after all these years of chasing me across the empire. You've got me. Have your revenge. What are you waiting for? Do it. Kill me. Do it!"

Tariq stood quickly. Kit wasn't cowed. He met Tariq's advance. Tariq's hands closed around his throat, smoke smoldering from his hot skin.

"You fucking bitch. I saved you, took you from that scorching hellhole, gave you everything, raised you, loved you. And you fucking betrayed me."

Kit choked out a laugh. He'd meant it to be mocking, but it was close to hysterical. He couldn't help it, it was either that or fall apart. Resentment churned his stomach. Too late. Tariq's comeuppance had come too late to save Kit.

"Love? Love." Kit wanted to scream, to throw things, to smash Tariq's face into a mess of cracked bones and broken teeth. He didn't want excuses, didn't want lies or for Tariq to act the noble philanthropist. "Fuck you! You turned me into a goddamned monster!"

"Don't you dare talk to me like that, you fucking bitch." Tariq's voice was low and dangerous, his fingers tightening, heat rising under his skin. "I lost everything. My estate. My money. My title. Command of my men. All for your hurt feelings. I did everything for you."

"Until I grew too old to hold your interest."

"Until you grew insolent and ungrateful and spoiled."

"You taught me well, Master."

Kit stared down at him. He could no longer see the man who had charmed him, who Kit had prized above all others. He was a pathetic, desperate, old man. Kit felt his hatred slide into indifference.

He threw Kit back. Kit stumbled, hitting his back on the tent pole, the canvas vibrating dangerously upon impact, but Kit didn't fall. He choked and got his breath back, rubbing his tender, burned throat and wincing.

"I thought to be merciful, to give you a chance to ask for forgiveness. I see I was wrong. You still need to be brought to heel. You will do as I command, Chris. You will regret betraying me."

Kit struggled to his feet, glaring defiantly at his former master when two men piled through the tent opening, weapons raised.

"You will, Chris, or I will kill Tallis."

"Then what leverage will you hold over me?" He left Tariq with a sneering smile as the Crows dragged him out and reaffixed the irons around his wrists and ankles.

Kit breathed out, his heart beating a painful rhythm against his ribs.

The Crow who'd escorted him returned. "What's this, Princess? Not to his taste anymore?"

Kit's muscles tensed along his spine.

"Leave him, Mark," one of the guarding Crows said.

Mark took hold of Kit's chains. "Come on, Princess, your chariot waits."

Kit held his ground, forcing Mark to stagger back.

"Now, now, Princess. Do as you're told." He gave Kit a heated up and down look. "You might have outgrown the general, but I'm sure there's someone here you can keep warm at night."

The other Crow stood close at Kit's back. "Take him back to the cart."

Mark's gaze flicked to his fellow soldier. "You want a sample, Joel? Didn't think you'd enjoy the taste of spoiled meat."

"Enough," the other Crow, Joel, snapped, his cheeks blushing.

Kit took a step toward Mark, softening his expression. Mark watched him, a smile creeping up his face. "That's it, Princess. My tent's nice and cozy."

Kit leaned in close, his cuffed hands reaching out and stroking the crow emblazoned on Mark's tunic. Kit wet his lips, his eyes on the man's mouth. Mark growled, low and lecherous. Smiling, Kit stroked the length of Mark's torso and groped his solid erection. With a snarl he gripped and pulled the man's bollocks, twisting savagely. Mark cried airlessly, curling in on himself. Kit grabbed his hair and swiftly brought his knee up, smashing it into the Crow's face.

Hands restrained him from behind. Shouting voices ordered to him to stop. Kit managed to get a few good kicks in before he was pulled away. Blood hot with rage, Kit fought all the way back to the cage, snarling incoherent curses at his captives. Threads of magic filled the air, but very attempt to siphon it left him reeling in pain.

Kit lay in his cage, shivering until the adrenaline subsided and he was left with nothing but silent misery. He breathed in deeply to quell the wave of emotion that hit like a storm when he thought of his former master, lost between the past and the present.

He could do nothing until he knew Harry's condition, until he was back with Kit.

Kit shuddered, ignoring the tears burning behind his eyes.

Chapter Ten

The entire time he and Harry were separated, Kit strained his ears, but he could hear nothing beyond the familiar rustling and orders of camping men. His side stung when he tried to reach out for any trace of Harry's magic, forcing him to his knees. He slid gracelessly down the bars of his prison, biting back burning tears.

It didn't stop him. Every few hours he slowed his breathing and reached out for Harry, for the darkness, the smallest sliver of magic enough to keep up his efforts, to know Harry was still alive, somewhere beyond his reach. He stopped fighting the pain of Tariq's brand, accepting it, welcoming it until it became a dull, constant ache. His skin was ablaze, but he wouldn't acknowledge it, didn't let it shake his determination. He ate and slept when he could, building his meager strength.

Harry was returned unceremoniously some days later. Kit went to him, glaring at the guards, some of whom pointed their weapons at him before the cage was locked and they backed off.

Left alone, Kit leaned in close, touching his cheek to Harry's. The fever had subsided. His color had returned, not the sickly red glow of fever, but the natural weather-worn blush of his skin. The bruises had turned a vivid green, the deeper ones still an ugly purple. His worst injuries had been tended to. They'd bathed and clothed him at least, in a thin tunic, and retied his hands, but this time in front, allowing him to lie comfortably on his back. His eyes were also uncovered.

"How are you feeling?" Kit asked gently.

Harry groaned, slowly opening his eyes, fixing his tired amber gaze on Kit. Could he see it? What Kit was? What he was going to do?

Harry said, "I do not approve of their bedside manner."

Kit chuckled, the smile painful. "Not up to your standards, Dr. Woodsman?" Harry's small smile was enough to reinforce his courage. He dipped and planted a soft kiss to Harry's dry lips, just a gentle press. Harry's lips gave the smallest push back. "Decided not to give up just yet?"

Harry looked searchingly into Kit's eyes. His bound hands reached up, cupping Kit's cheek. Kit leaned into his touch, kissing his palm. Harry didn't say anything, his eyes sad and defeated. Kit's hope deflated. He summoned a bitter grin. "You may want to die, but I'm not going to fucking give in to them. I have no desire to let Tariq win."

"Kit."

"No," he growled, clinging fiercely to Harry. "I've survived everything. I'm not going to give up because you fucking have."

"Kit," Harry said softly, his fingers stroking Kit's jaw, his eyes pained.

Kit's eyes stung. His cheeks were hot. He sat back on his heels and turned away from Harry, ashamed.

* * * *

Their journey continued. The green forests opened out into wide grasslands, following old merchant paths from when the village of Paix was once on the outskirts of a large port city, long before war broke out, severing ancient trading lines between the two territories and reducing the thriving population severely. From there they made the hazardous journey down the cliff face, descending the twisting path that had been hand-carved into the white rock many centuries before. Barely used, the path was unkept, worn away by storms and sea, crumbling in places.

The cage, deemed too heavy to risk the trip, was abandoned and Kit and Harry were forced to hobble down the ancient path wearing their weighty iron bracelets. With Kit's arms restrained behind his back, it made for an even more terrifying descent. Harry kept a firm hold on the back of Kit's shirt with his manacled hands. The Crows were too preoccupied with their own safety to offer them more than cursory glances. Kit suspected they were envious of not having their own partner to cling to as they peered down at the far-off beach below.

Inevitably, one Crow lost his footing as the stone cracked and gave way. To save himself he grabbed the soldier at his side. It did no good. They both fell over the ledge, screaming all the way down. Harry seized and pinned Kit to the cliff face with his body.

By the time the rest of the party reached the rocky beach, the bodies were already swarmed by carrion vultures. Outraged, one of the Crows yelled and threatened the large birds, gun raised. The great birds cawed in annoyance but quickly settled back over their prize when Tariq admonished the man for wasting time. It earned him a few miserable or disgusted looks from the men, but no one argued.

The Crows made camp farther up the beach near the remains of the ancient port to wait for the morning, when a vessel from the capital would come for them.

A stake was beaten deep into the compact sand, to which Kit and Harry were tied. When food came, Harry was able to feed himself. He gathered the dried strips of meat, sharing them out equally. They had not spoken since Kit's outburst, but at night they still nestled together. It was better now Harry could hold Kit in his arms again. Harry huddled close, offering the dried meat to Kit. Kit opened his mouth and bit into the tacky flesh and tore it off. Harry gave him a satisfied nod, reminding Kit of Harry's doctoral treatment. He allowed himself to smile at the bittersweet memories as he watched Harry tuck into his own portion.

Any animosity between them disappeared with that shared meal. No. There never had been any animosity. Despite all the ill Kit had brought to Harry, he was forever patient, forever caring, and Kit felt like the spoiled brat Tariq had accused him of being.

It was time to return the favor, though he doubted Harry would see it that way when it was over.

After their meal, Kit leaned into Harry, clumsily burying his face against Harry's throat and breathed, "I know I have no right to this, but I need your trust."

Harry rested his hands on Kit's chest, over his heart. "I do trust you."

Kit chuffed, nuzzling closer still. "I am unworthy, but thank you, and I'm sorry for my words before. The thought of you dying does not sit well with me."

Harry brushed Kit's lips with his thumb. Kit closed his eyes and kissed the callused pad.

"With that, I'm sorry I must do this."

"What?"

Kit didn't answer. He didn't need to. He saw the horror cloud Harry's face as he pulled on the shadowy thread of power pulsing weakly from within Harry.

Kit gritted his teeth against the scream trying to escape him. The brand on his hip flared hot as though it were burning into his flesh anew.

"Kit... Stop," Harry breathed, writhing in his restraints.

He couldn't. Even if he wanted to, he couldn't. Harry's power was filling him, coursing through his veins, chilling the burn of Tariq's mark in his skin.

Tariq's voice rang out. "Get Leonor. Now!"

Two Crows ran across the beach, weapons drawn. One of them was the Crow from the other night, Joel. He hesitated, staring down as Kit glared at them, daring them closer with bared teeth as Harry's magic polluted his body, eager to escape, pushing at the edges of his will.

"Now!" Tariq bellowed.

Kit hissed through clenched teeth, "If you want to live, run."

Joel flinched. The other Crow's face hardened and he gripped Kit's arm and the collar of his shirt, forcing him forward as his irons were freed from the stake. Released, Kit fell to the ground, sand filling his teeth and sticking to his lips. His brand flared hot. He felt Harry fighting him, and Tariq's presence nudging the edges of his mind. The thread severed under their dual resistance. Kit squirmed and clutched his hip, snarling against the scream wanting to rip from his throat.

"Kit!"

It was Harry.

Stay away. Let me finish this. I promise we'll be safe.

He could do this. He had to.

"Kit!"

"Keep Tallis away."

He'd followed Kit, fighting the Crows to get to him.

No, Harry, you idiot. Stay away.

Heavy heat pressed in around him and Harry's bound hands clutched his shirt. "Leave him be. Get back." Harry's voice was thick and harsh against Kit's ear. He wouldn't let go.

"Enough. Bring them here," Tariq growled.

The warmth left Kit. Harry's fingers pulled as they were ripped from Kit's shirt. The smell of his master's jasmine perfume tickled his nose, clogging his throat as he breathed. Brought within a couple feet of Tariq, Kit was forced to his knees. He heard Harry protesting, but didn't dare look back.

"Unbind Leonor."

No one moved.

"Sir, is that wise?" a Crow asked from behind Kit.

"Do it."

Kit kept his eyes on Tariq, seething and steeling himself for what was to come. With a short series of clicks, his wrists were freed from the irons. He clenched his teeth as his stiff muscles protested up and down his arms.

Tariq fixed his gaze on Kit. He breathed in deep and the air changed around him. "*Obey me.*"

The attack against his will was so sudden, his body so weak, Kit couldn't muster the strength to repel Tariq's violation. It filled him, a deep burning, a tongue of white-hot flame searing through his muscles, scoring bone. Gritting his teeth, Kit summoned all his strength to fight, to pull free of Tariq's grip. Pain ripped through his side, the brand scorching his hip as fresh as the day it had been carved into his flesh. No art, no skill, only pain and suffering.

Kit collapsed forward. He was screaming.

Tariq's blurry visage grew closer. "*Obey me.*"

Limbs shuddering, Kit threw himself back, trying to escape. He clutched the sides of his head as though he could block Tariq's influence. Through strangled screams, Kit heard a voice calling to him. It was Harry, shouting his name.

He buried his face in his hands. *Don't look.* He didn't want Harry to see him like this, didn't want Harry to see his resistance snap, when Tariq entered his mind, controlling him like a marionette on a string.

Harry's voice cut out. Kit strained to hear him, to feel Harry's presence, his body convulsing. A scuffle had broken out. Men were rushing behind Kit. Harry was fighting to get to him.

"Keep him restrained," Tariq ordered. It momentarily weakened his control and Kit pushed back against that small chink. A sudden, violent pressure landed on his chest. Winded, he grabbed at

Tariq's ankle. Tariq stomped on him again. *"Obey me, Chris!"*

A wailing scream ripped from Kit's throat. His grip slipped from his control. White-hot flame consumed him from within. He gave in to the pain, tears pouring from his eyes, enveloped in Tariq's command.

I'm sorry, Harry.

It took four men to bring Harry down. They kicked and wrestled him to the ground, tried to force a harsh gag into his mouth when he wouldn't stop screaming for Kit, but Harry bit and spat at them, receiving a sharp back-handed slap for his efforts. He could do nothing but watch, impotent, as Kit's body was wracked with spasms, his eyes rolling back in his head when Tariq finally lifted his boot off Kit's chest.

Harry blinked and was no longer on a beach surrounded by Crows. He was on a foreign battlefield, watching Louis being gunned down in the throes of terrified madness.

"Rise," Tariq ordered.

Like a rag doll hoisted on invisible strings, Kit's body rose from the ground, standing before Tariq. All around, the men stood in perfect, awed silence. They looked upon Kit with wide-eyed fear.

Kit's eyes were lifeless, his face a mask, as though he had never smiled. Harry tried to recall the mischievous joy dancing behind those blue eyes, the softness of his mouth, now cut to a hard, mirthless line. It was as though Kit had never wept in pain or laughed in delight. There was nothing, a gaping void where life should have been. What stood now was merely a puppet. Kit's flesh, but not his soul.

"General, I don't think—"

"Silence!" Tariq's voice rang out, too loud in the startled quiet of the clearing. "Now, Christopher, see what happens when you misbehave."

"General!"

"I said be quiet!"

The Crow shrank back, looking from Tariq to Kit, fearful.

Tariq leaned in close and said softly, *"Christopher, kill Henry Tallis."*

Kit's blind gaze shifted. He turned and looked upon Harry with dead eyes. Harry's breath caught as he watched Kit approach, his gait smooth and purposeful, his face devoid of any consciousness, his stare blank and hooded. He was calm, showing no cognizance of what he was being compelled to do, which disturbed Harry most of all.

"Kit," Harry breathed.

Kit stopped. A flicker of eyelashes. Kit opened his mouth. A slow breath shuddered past his lips.

The men holding Harry tensed. "General," one said in warning.

Tariq ignored him. *"Do it, Christopher."*

Harry tried to summon a smile for Kit. Tears welled and tracked down Kit's cheeks, his face so young and vulnerable Harry's heart contracted. "It's all right, Kit."

"Shut him up." At Tariq's order, knuckles smashed into Harry's temple, snapping his head to the side. His vision darkened around the edges.

Kit stiffened, his brow creasing.

"Christopher!" Tariq bellowed.

"Kit," Harry said softly, slurring a little, pushing past the aching throb inside his skull. "It's okay."

Kit whimpered and fell to his knees inches from Harry. The Crows holding Harry flinched back. Harry shrugged out of their startled grip. They didn't fight him.

A sheen of tears glistened over Kit's eyes. A choked sob erupted from his lips. He was fighting Tariq so hard. Veins protruded under his flushing skin, his breathing coming in sharp gasps, muscles flexing in his jaw, his pain gutting Harry.

Harry addressed Tariq. "Stop this. You're pulling him apart."

Tariq didn't look at him, his teeth clenched, his brow gleaming with sweat.

Another sob tore from Kit, tears tracking down his cheeks. "H-Harry..." His lips strained into a painful grimace. "I can't...control... It's too strong... Kill them all."

Panic gripped Harry. "Tariq, please, stop this."

"I said shut him up!"

No one moved on his order.

Kit raised a shaking hand, reaching out for Harry. "No! Don't..." Harry grunted, his face wet with tears.

Kit's trembling palm pressed against Harry's chest, over his heart. Harry couldn't move. A hollow vacuum drew the darkness from its carefully guarded cage and his breath froze in his chest. It was nothing like the first time Kit had drawn on his power. He couldn't breathe, his mouth gaping soundlessly.

Kit's grimace contorted his beauty, his blue eyes drowning in glittering tears. He panted and swayed back and forth on his knees, his body wracked with tremors, his hand never moving from Harry's chest.

"*Chris! Enough!*" Tariq yelled, his voice hitched with panic.

Kit snarled, teeth clenched, grabbing his wrist with his free hand, holding it in place. The darkness continued to pour from Harry and spill over into Kit. Harry felt his resistance, his struggle for release. It was too much. He wouldn't be able to control it.

"No," Harry grunted. "Run!"

There was a shift in the Crows. They looked about, waiting for the first man to move.

"Stay where you are," Tariq ordered, shrieking as he stared wide-eyed between Kit and Harry.

"Harry," Kit breathed. "I c-can't control it. It's so dark...so cold."

"Kit," Harry said. "I know, but you have to try or all these men will die."

He shook his head and growled, "They deserve it. They hurt people. They hurt you."

It was the Madness. Harry remembered the glorious, momentary taste of justice as he had brought down those men who had taken Louis from him. But he also knew the lack of control, the horror and the heavy guilt of every life lost that day still weighed on him. "They don't deserve this, Kit. You don't want their blood on your hands."

Kit's eyes opened, his gaze unfocused. "What are a few more lives to me?"

"Kit, please. Don't let them turn you into a killer."

Kit choked a painful laugh, his voice thin. "Too late for that." He leaned in close to Harry, closing his eyes.

"Kit, no." Harry looked to the Crows. "Run! Now! Go!"

The men started to abandon the beach, making their way back to the cliff face. They'd never make it. Harry heard the drawing of weapons. It was useless. They couldn't stop this. Harry grabbed Kit, hugged him close, unable to do anything else.

A gun was primed somewhere in the swelling chaos. Harry tensed.

"Take him down!"

"Wait! Stop!" Tariq cried from somewhere beyond their embrace.

A gun exploded, its song deafening the chaos of shouting men. The thud of a bullet burying itself into flesh stopped Harry's heart. Kit collapsed in Harry's arms.

No. No.

Harry gathered Kit close to him, a great quaking sob ripping from his chest, each heaved breath a painful compression around his chest.

The drain on the darkness did nothing to diminish its swell churning inside him, drawing on his grief and his rage and gathering malevolence until it was spilling from his pores. He didn't tell them to run this time. He looked over Kit's shoulder at each man, daring them to run. He would kill them all.

But the Crows weren't running. They were staring at Tariq. He lay on the sandy ground. Blood sprayed in great gouts from the bullet wound ripped through his throat.

"Harry..."

Harry almost swallowed his tongue, pulling Kit up and holding him at arm's length, his eyes raking over his body. He was whole, exhausted, his face ashen and shining with sweat, but he was alive.

"Harry, he's gone. He's not in my head. He's gone."

"Kit..."

It was too late. The darkness pumped out of him, the first wave sweeping over the men closest.

The change was instantaneous. The Madness erupted from Harry. It took all of Kit's remaining energy to counter the dark magic and protect himself from the effects. It scratched at his weakened barriers. The chorus of chaos grew from a rumble to a roar as horror broke out around them.

Men were screaming, others running in fear, weapons drawn, cutting down wide-eyed men without prejudice.

Kit watched in horror as the frenzy reached the men fleeing up the beach toward the cliff. They were clutching their heads or falling to their knees, contorting and shrieking as the darkness enclosed them in fear and madness.

The crowd around them was erupting into a bloodbath. Kit had seen death, served as its harbinger under Tariq's order, but it had been swift and clean. This was hell on earth. Men pulling apart their fellow soldiers with nothing but their hands. Beating their heads against rocks until their skulls split open, spilling forth mashed gray matter. Cutting off their flesh and limbs and feasting on them as they bled out. Screaming as they were dragged to the sea and held down below the water. Kit averted his eyes from the chaos.

"Harry." He cupped Harry's face in his hands. Harry's eyes were dull, seeing none of the anarchy. "Harry. You have to stop." He'd wanted this, wanted Harry's power to ravage the band of Crows so they could escape, but now he couldn't stand it. He hadn't understood the horror Harry had been holding back.

Harry met his gaze, silent tears spilling from his eyes. "I can't."

"Yes, you can. You fucking can. You have to." He pressed his forehead to Harry's, ignoring the tremors shaking his hands.

"Kit," Harry breathed. Kit barely heard him through the chaos surrounding them. He reached up and gripped the back of Kit's neck and drew him close, his lips against Kit's ear. "It's too late. I can't stop it. But you can."

"What do you mean? How?"

Harry's grip tightened. Kit winced. "Kill me."

Kit gripped back. "We've already had this conversation," he said through a tight smile, swallowing hard. "I won't do it."

"Look around. This won't stop until every man is dead. Or I am."

A dark part of Kit's soul said good riddance to the shadow that had plagued him for years. But he couldn't bring himself to look back at the frenzied bloodbath, blood tainting the air and voided bowls polluting the sand.

"Please, Kit." Harry's voice broke, his tears soaking Kit's shoulder. "End this."

A painful gagging lump in Kit's throat stopped his refusal. He clutched Harry, stealing his warmth and his strength. "You can't ask this of me. I...I... You can't make me do this." He closed his eyes, tears chilling on his cheeks. "I love you."

Harry tensed under his hold. A warm shuddering exhalation gusted over Kit's neck, making him shiver, but he pressed in closer, breathing him in. "Then do this for me, please. We're running out of time."

Kit couldn't get warm, his skin erupting with gooseflesh. He couldn't get close enough to Harry, couldn't pull heat from his body. Nuzzling from

Harry's neck to his lips, he softly pressed his mouth to Harry's salty, tear-stained cheeks along the way. Pulling back, he looked into Harry's dark, watery gaze. "Close your eyes."

Harry did, the relief in his smile so potent Kit's heart constricted. He kissed Harry again. He deepened it, Harry stiffening in his arms as he slipped his tongue inside, opening Harry up to him. He concentrated on the Madness, on the darkness pouring from Harry. He drew it in, letting it fill his mouth, his senses, taking it in deep. The cold, dark magic sliced through him, filling his core, the power endless and infinite, wanting to be unleashed, wanting to destroy. That intoxicating and shattering rush sent his blood surging cold and fast through his veins, infusing his body with overwhelming power.

Harry tensed. Kit held him firm, glad for once that Harry couldn't use his strength to fight him. Harry mumbled something, an incoherent protest into the kiss, but Kit wouldn't let go, not until he'd taken as much as he could.

"Kit, stop."

Kit clutched Harry's throat, the back of his head, drawing in more and more. It was bottomless, no longer a struggle, a ceaseless fount pouring into him, willingly entering and filling the vessel inside him. Across the beach, the men's screaming had ceased as the magic retreated, as Kit pulled it into himself. It would have been so easy, so simple to release it, let it tear the world apart and watch helplessly, but he held onto it.

Harry turned his lips away. "Stop. You can't control it."

The connection broke. Kit pushed Harry back. He went falling onto his ass, limp and aghast as he stared at Kit, eyes wide with fear.

Kit tried to get away, to get to his feet. He crumpled, collapsing forward, hugging his chest.

"Kit."

"Stay back." He heaved. The darkness engulfed him, fighting to be free, slamming against his skull, trembling through his limbs, constricting his heart, swelling inside his lungs. Oh God, he couldn't hold it. It was too strong, more powerful than any magic he'd ever wielded.

"Kit, stop."

Kit blocked him out, blocked out everything. He needed to focus, needed to bend and change the dark madness. He thought of the maelstrom he'd unleashed inside Harry's cabin and the destruction it had wrought when he'd syphoned a single touch of Harry's magic. He was running out of time, the magic longing to be free from the frail shell of his body. Gritting his teeth, molars aching, he fought the urge to vomit.

With a gurgling grunt he threw his fist at the earth. The immense flow of power pumped from him in waves into the bloodied sand.

Almost blind with tears, Kit watched the sparse tufts of long grass shrivel and brown atop the beach, drying and crackling under the wispy sea breeze. Grunting, Kit shuddered, muscles locking as the darkness pushed against his skin. He kept a stranglehold on the magic, felt it spill nonetheless, despite his best efforts. The darkness expanded, spreading out across the beach, killing the grass, climbing through rock pools, the gathered clumps of seaweed shriveling into twisted gray wisps before crumbling to dust. Tiny crabs scuttled from their hiding places only to collapse like empty suits of armor. Clams and mussels clapped furiously before falling deadly silent, their shells splintering and crumbling into sand. Farther off a putrid smell wafted from the sea. Countless fish and other small sea creatures surfaced and bobbed lifelessly atop the murky, putrid water, the calm waves regurgitating and leaving their small, shriveled bodies along the shoreline.

"Kit!"

He couldn't stop it. Fear surged through his veins. Death and disease spread farther along the beach. He looked up, seeing Harry's stricken face through a blur of tears. "I'm sorry, Harry."

"No. No, no, no. Give it back. Give it back to me."

Kit managed a tight smile through his straining grimace. "I'm sorry."

Harry lurched forward, taking hold of Kit's shoulders. Drained, exhausted, Kit collapsed against Harry, shuddering.

The magic slipped from him, eager to return home.

"It's all right. I've got it. I've got you."

Kit clung to Harry, exhausted and trembling uncontrollably.

New magic filtered through Kit's waning consciousness. Kit tensed, was ready to attack when his body grew too heavy to fight. His mind slowed, lulled into much-welcome rest. He watched the first shards of sunlight break over the cliff edge, lighting the beach, glistening off the sea surface. He wanted to watch the spectacle a little longer, but his vision darkened and the light disappeared altogether.

Chapter Eleven

Dizziness swarmed Harry's mind, he couldn't seem to focus on anything. He'd tried opening his eyes, but couldn't summon the strength. He could smell the sea, taste the salt in the air. Blood and decay mingled with the scents of brine and dusty sand. His body ached all over. He longed to lie still and sleep for a year, but something wouldn't let him. He swayed to and fro. Heaving breaths and grunts sounded around him. For a while he was almost vertical, but weightless. He couldn't figure out how the world was now slanted at an angle. He was neither standing nor lying down. He wanted to ask, but only a soft moan came up his throat.

He slipped away into darkness. Kit was there, naked, his limbs jerking as though invisible strings from above dragged him about. His face was pulled into a mad smile, bright pink dots painted on his cheeks, his eyes blank and staring, and he was screaming.

* * * *

Harry woke with a painful jolt, blinking rapidly into the blazing light filtering through a canopy of leaves. The pure blue of the sky behind them was too bright. He shut his eyes. "Kit?" His voice was little more than a dry heave. "Kit?" he tried again.

A rush of voices came, incoherent to Harry's ears. Then one came through. "It's all right, Doc. He's safe."

Something came back to Harry and a film of tears wet his eyes. "No. He was shot."

"Nothing like that, Doc. I promise. He's just sleeping, same as you should be. Quiet now. We're almost home."

Harry tried to shake his head, his throat too thick to form words. He remembered the smell of death, but couldn't hold onto the thought long enough before falling once more into darkness. It wasn't the terrifying darkness of his nightmares, but the welcome pull and mindlessness of peaceful, dreamless sleep.

* * * *

The swaying had stopped, so had the distant rumbling of men moving about him. No voices now, only the gently hum of far-off wildlife in the trees.

He was in bed. He was home. He breathed in deeply, smelling the tallow soap on his pillow, and felt the worn scratch of his blankets and the pool of heat coming in through the small window.

Wood creaked around him. It was familiar and safe. Then someone cleared their throat. Harry's eyes shot open and he peered about, glad he hadn't been dreaming. He really was home. His eyes landed on a familiar face, strange though it was to see it inside his house.

Harry struggled to sit up.

"Whoa there," Thom said, helping Harry sit up when his arms failed to hold him.

"Thom, what are you doing here?"

"Keeping watch over you." Thom propped the pillow against the headboard so Harry could rest against it. "Well, both of you."

At Harry's puzzled squint, Thom gestured to Harry's left. Harry swallowed as he took in Kit. He was mostly sitting in a chair, but his chest was lying across the bed, head resting on his folded arm, fast asleep. One hand was stretched out as though he'd been clutching Harry's. Harry's chest swelled. He reached out and brushed the fallen hair away from Kit's sleeping eyes. His lashes twitched a little, but he didn't stir.

"Poor lad. Hasn't left your side."

Harry forced his gaze back to Thom. "What happened? How did we get back here? How did — "

"Easy, Doc," Thom said in hushed tones, gesturing again to Kit's sleeping form. "Celeste came to me a few nights back, saying you went haring out of her house like hellfire was on your heels. I gathered a few volunteers to come and see what was happening. By the time we got here the place was empty, but we noticed blood on the floor and signs of a fire outside. Luckily Cole, you know, the fishmonger's father, was a fair tracker back in his army days. Bit rusty, but we managed to follow your path through the forest."

"You found us?"

"Yep."

Harry stared, astonished. "But — "

"It's all right, lad," Thom said with a soft smile, cutting Harry off.

"It's not." Harry clenched his fists around the blanket. "I could have killed you all. You had no idea what you were walking into."

"I had a fair idea when I learned the Blue Crows were out looking for you."

When Harry remained silent, unsure how much he could explain, Thom sighed and started plucking at the buttons of his cuff. Once the cuff was open, he rolled up his sleeve and held up his hand. A perfect 'W' was scored into the flesh below his wrist.

"Been a bloody long time since I served. Tariq was just a green cadet when I met him, can't believe he made it so high up the ranks. Then again, the Crows aren't what they used to be."

"What do you mean?" Harry asked, taking his eyes off the brand.

"Do you know any witch that would sooner use a gun than his magic? I don't."

Harry gave a shrug then winced. "I don't know. I didn't serve in the Witch Army."

"Then I'll tell you. None, unless they'd been tethered. Those lads on the beach, they weren't witches. No more so than Tariq was a general."

Harry closed his eyes, his head throbbing, unable to understand what Thom was telling him.

"The night those Crows came to the village, some came to the Swan. I didn't want any trouble, so I kept their drinks free and full the entire night. Men start to talk when they've had one too many, especially men with a grievance. They told me about the Crows and about Tariq. Turns out Tariq was disgraced and had been stripped of his rank."

"Why?"

"Didn't get into too much detail before a fight broke out between the Crows, or whoever they were, and some of the regulars they were hassling."

Harry continued to stare at him, struggling to keep up. His head pounded and he just wanted to close his eyes. "So what were they doing here if they weren't sent by the emperor?"

"Think you should ask your man next to you when he wakes up. Poor lad."

Harry looked to Kit and felt a protective jolt in his chest. Looking back at Thom, he said, "Did you... You stopped it. You stopped the M— My magic."

Thom shook his head. "Don't know nothing about that. You two were already out of it by the time we made it down that bloody cliff."

"What about Tariq?"

"Dead. Killed by his own men as far as I could tell. Put him down with a bullet to the throat. Doesn't surprise me though."

"Why'd you say that?"

Thom blew out a sigh, ruffling his mustache. "He was some noble's son. Thought he could get away with anything, that and with his ability to wield an element." Thom shook his head again. "It was hard to argue with him. I was long gone before he ever got into command, but I can bet he didn't come by it fairly."

"And the Cro—" Harry swallowed. "Those men?"

"Dead."

"Oh God." Harry's chest tightened.

Thom clutched his shoulder. "Don't waste your grief on them. If they put their lot in with Tariq they were the lowest of scoundrels, mark my words."

"Doesn't mean I had the right to kill them."

"Men like that, they're the sort of villains that walk through life with death haunting their shadow. If it hadn't been you, it would have been someone else, more than likely from the end of a short length of rope."

Harry shook his head, unable to believe that, shocked that such harsh words were coming from kind, welcoming Thom who he'd never heard say a bad word about anyone. Though he obviously didn't really know the man as well as he thought, as he watched Thom unroll his sleeve and fasten his cuff.

A murmured, sleepy moan came from the other side of the bed. Harry stared down at Kit, remembering the pain in his eyes as he'd fought against Tariq's hold.

"It may not seem like it now, but you two are safe here, lad, safe because you protected him. Don't think for a second that your life meant less than those men's. Regret leads to despair and we can't do without you, you hear?"

Harry had to clear his throat before he could speak, and even then his voice was thick with emotion. "Thank you, Thom."

Thom gripped his shoulder. "It was nothing, lad. After all you've done for us, it was the least we could do. We outcasts have to stick together." He thumped Harry on the back, making him wince. His face grew somber and he said, "I'm serious, Harry, whatever you may have done in the past, you've done good work here and you're always welcome."

Harry swallowed, looking away. He nodded and Thom took it as a sign to leave with a final clap to Harry's back.

Harry looked to Kit again, still sleeping soundly at his side. He didn't dare dream or hope that he was finally, truly free. His past would always haunt him.

But right now, seeing Kit's peaceful expression, Harry wanted nothing more than to slip inside that peace along with him. He shimmied back down, trying his best not to disturb Kit. He stroked his knuckles along Kit's cheek, noting the faint bruising. A spark of rage quickened Harry's heart, but his eyes were growing heavy with every blink. He placed his hand on Kit's and let his eyes close.

* * * *

When he woke again, Kit wasn't next to him. The bed was cold. With some effort, Harry pushed himself up to his elbows, making the bed creak. Heart swelling in his chest, he found Kit standing farther off, his back to Harry.

"I found your supply of powders and concoctions," Kit said without turning. He stood next to a small chest of drawers. Atop it were three bottles, a jug and cup. "I didn't dare administer one without your knowledge. The last thing I want to do is poison you."

"The one on the far left is for pain."

Kit finally turned and held the cup and bottle so Harry could see. "Say when."

"When."

Something was wrong. Kit looked lost. He wore the same expression Harry had seen when Kit had first entered his home, guarded and afraid. Kit was silent as he stirred the mixture, his focus solely fixed on the cup. When he finally went to Harry, his gaze was distant.

"Here," he said. Instead of offering him the cup, Kit gently helped him sit up straight and brought the cup to his lips. Harry took hold of his wrist as he swallowed down the gritty, bitter solution, trying to catch Kit's gaze, but he stubbornly avoided looking Harry directly in the eye. "Thank you."

Kit gave a vague smile, finally meeting Harry's gaze. It was only a flicker, but it was enough for Harry to read the pain there. "We seem to have exchanged roles, Dr. Woodsman." Kit tentatively reached out wiped his thumb along Harry's lower lip.

"Kit," Harry said, taking hold of Kit's hand, lacing their fingers together. He swallowed and asked, "Who are you?"

There was a held breath of sorrow, but Kit hid it with a long sigh and a hollow chuckle. "I thought you didn't need to know who I am."

"Kit." Harry held on tight to the swell of emotions and cleared his throat. "Please, I need to know. I need to know you're safe."

Kit's eyes widened, then he shook his head. "You are a wonder, Dr. Woodsman."

Harry gently pulled until Kit sat on the bed next to him. Kit looked lost again, his hand shaking a little in Harry's. "My name is Christopher Leonor, former citizen of Rasacara. I was a soldier, recruited by the Blue Crows when I was twelve."

"*Twelve?*"

"Yes. It's not uncommon. Tariq found me in a cell in Pechic, a small market town in northern Rasacara. I was a pickpocket. My powers manifested for the first time when a city guard caught me. He was the first but definitely not the last man I killed. Tariq took me under his wing, testing the limits of my power. He fed and clothed me, let me stay in the officers' barracks, which were much nicer than the cadets'. I even visited his family estate on occasion. I ate rich food I had never heard of, wore grand clothes tailor-made for me. I slept in huge beds with soft sheets. I had servants who answered to my every desire, so long as Tariq approved." Kit cast his sight into the distance, his voice deceptively light and casual even as his eyes grew darker. "He taught me to fight and I was good at it. Tariq liked to keep me close, liked to show me off to his wealthy friends. My power, my skill with a blade, anything they wanted."

Harry had a sick, twisting feeling growing in his gut. "What happened?"

"I don't know if I like this inquisitive side of you." Kit was smiling, but his eyes were sorrowful.

"Sorry, I shouldn't have—"

Kit shrugged. "You're curious. It's only natural." His Adam's apple bobbed in his throat. "He kept me close until I grew too old to satisfy him."

Harry's stomach churned and his heart raced with fury.

Kit didn't look at him, his hands fidgeting in his lap. "I should have known the end was coming. I was almost sixteen, far too old to keep him interested. But..." He gasped as though trying not to be sick. "I thought I was different. He made me feel special."

"Kit, stop, you don't have to tell me any more." He wasn't sure how much more of it he could hear without rising and leaving to go and break something. He'd never felt rage like it. Even when Louis had lain dying in his arms, pain and grief had overridden his anger.

A chilling wave swept under his skin, the darkness answering his fury.

Kit turned to Harry and placed a hand over his chest, stroking small circles over his heart. Leaning in close, he said softly, "It's all right. It was a long time ago. Calm down."

Harry breathed deep and closed his eyes. Miraculously, the darkness slipped back under the surface, like a dragon being soothed to sleep by a lullaby. Harry opened his eyes, heart pounding. "Kit," he uttered, chest heaving, trying to contain the swell of emotion in his chest. "How?"

"While you slept you had nightmares. Your magic stirred, but when I touched you, talked to you, it stopped. If I had to guess, I think your power is connected to your emotional state. Whenever you're in distress or angry or hurt, it manifests to protect you."

Harry held Kit's hand against his chest, breathing more easily. "It can't be." But it was. He felt it now, the easing of his heart, the quieting of his rage and the darkness slinking back. After all these years alone and in fear, fighting the darkness back... Was it really so simple? He shuddered and gripped Kit's hand tighter, his heart pounding, tears welling in his eyes. He closed them, fought back the tears. He needed to listen to Kit, to be there for him, to understand. He breathed in deeply then nodded to Kit. He was calm, the darkness quiet now.

Kit continued as though the darkness hadn't interrupted, as though he hadn't just offered Harry a sense of monumental salvation. "I know how foolish and naïve I was. I didn't understand at the time how wrong it was. I had everything I'd ever wanted, so it seemed a small price to pay."

"My God, Kit," Harry said.

Kit swallowed again, his eyes focused on some memory, then cleared his throat. When he spoke again, his words were strained with withheld tears. "He used me, used my power as a conduit for magic, and made me his weapon. I killed tens and hundreds of men for him. Enemies, allies, anyone he thought had slighted him in some way. But the worst part is, toward the end, he didn't need to use my power to control me. I did those things. I killed willingly for him, for his attention, for his love, and I did it all without pity or remorse. I was his creature, his monster."

"Kit, you were only a child." Harry reached for him, but Kit resisted, the line of his back rigid.

He shook his head. It took a long time until he was ready to continue. "Then the war ended. The last stronghold in Rasacara fell." Kit exhaled shakily, getting his voice back under control. "I was free and had no idea who I was or what I should do. I was once more that scared boy back in that cell in Pechic, but this time the door was open to me and I could walk free. I ran before he could throw me away."

Harry had to clear his throat. "But he came after you."

"Before I left, I sent letters to the emperor. Tariq corresponded with him directly so I knew how to reach him. I wrote of my own experience and rumors I had heard but ignored for the longest time. I sent lists of Tariq's expenses, money he used for his own vices, which the empire was inadvertently funding. I told of the powerful, sordid men Tariq associated with. Anything that I knew would hurt him. I never knew if these letters made it to the emperor or if he would read them, let alone act on them. But he did and Tariq was ruined.

"It was some years until Tariq tracked me down. I found employment as a noble lady's bodyguard. When she betrayed me it felt, inevitably, like my punishment. We fought and Tariq attempted to bind my magic, but I got away." His voice wavered. "I should have run sooner. I had the means all along, but I was more scared of losing his love above anything else. He was all I'd known for so long. It was only when he began pushing me away that I acted out of spite."

Harry pulled him into an embrace, heedless of Kit's resistance, stroking his hands firmly up and down Kit's back as if he were cold. "You are not responsible for those deaths. It was Tariq, only Tariq, and now he's dead. You are free."

Kit's breath caught. He gave a strangled sob then buried his face into Harry's shoulder. He wept silently, soaking Harry's shirt. Even when Kit ran out of tears, Harry didn't let him go, holding him, hand massaging his nape. After a time, Kit pulled back and pressed a soft, tear-stained kiss on Harry's lips. "Thank you."

"I did nothing."

Kit shook his head then pressed his forehead to Harry's. "No. You saved me. Not just from the Crows. You ended my life of death and destruction the day you ended the war."

Harry grunted in pain. "No, there was nothing good about that day."

Kit gripped his face, pressed more wet kisses to Harry's cheeks, brow and eyelids, his lips never leaving Harry's skin. "You ended the war. You saved countless lives."

"By killing hundreds of men."

"Men who would have died anyway."

Harry shook his head. "You can't know that."

"True, but I am grateful to you nonetheless. So are all those men across the empire who made it back to their families, who now live in a time of peace."

"Don't," Harry protested, trying to turn his face away from Kit's affection. "I don't deserve—"

Kit silenced him with another kiss on the mouth. Harry shuddered as he fought back tears, feeling Kit's thumb brushing them aside regardless. "What of young Davy Junior, or his twin sister, or all the others you have saved, all the people that love you? Surely you have done enough to earn absolution?"

Was it enough? He wanted it to be enough, to be forgiven. How could one weigh the lives of so many men against the lives of others? "I don't know."

"Then you have to keep going, you have to live on and continue your work, keep saving lives until you've done enough. I'll help you."

Harry froze and looked up into Kit's face, the honest determination and love in his eyes almost stopping Harry's heart. He combed his fingers through Kit's hair then stroked the length of his neck, feeling the steady pound of his heartbeat under warm skin. "That could take a very long time."

"I know."

"So you'll stay?"

Kit gave a half smile. "As long as you'll have me."

"Always," Harry said, drawing Kit into another kiss, falling back onto the pillows, pulling Kit down atop him.

With careful hands, Kit slowly stripped off the little Harry was wearing, gentle and slow, their kiss never breaking. Harry rose up to help, his hands going for Kit's clothes. Naked, Kit slipped into bed alongside him, their bodies pressed together so close, sharing every breath, hands stroking and groping and gripping so tight Harry lost all sense of the outside world. He was locked together with Kit, unable to hold him tight enough, unable to count every heartbeat, to draw in enough of his scent. Kit was just as hungry, just as greedy as their kisses deepened and sweat mingled between their hot, airless skin.

Kit was alive. He was staying. None of it seemed real, even as he pulled Kit close, breathing him in. His heart thudded almost painfully with newfound joy. It was all too much and not enough at the same time.

"Kit," he breathed between kisses.

Kit offered a mumbled moan in response.

"Kit, I want..." Harry couldn't say the words, too breathless, his face heating as he shifted to spread his legs, catching Kit between them, thrusting to rub his cock against Kit's equally eager length.

Breathing hard, Kit finally broke free just enough to meet Harry's gaze. His cheeks were flushed red, his eyes bright and his hair a mess from Harry continuously running his fingers through it. "Harry, are you sure?"

Harry leaned up and kissed him again, tightening his thighs around Kit. He nipped at Kit's lower lip before pulling back and smiling, his embarrassment gone. "Yes. I want you."

Kit's astonished brow furrowed a little.

"What is it?"

"You're not saying this because of what I told you? Pitying me?"

Harry pushed up onto his elbows. "God, no, Kit. Never. It's what I want. But if you don't—"

"Sorry. No. I want that too. I'm sorry. I've ruined it."

Harry took him into his arms and pressed his lips to Kit's neck. "Nothing's ruined. I just want to be with you, however I can. I love you."

He felt Kit's chest expand under his hold. Kit dropped his head to Harry's shoulder and breathed in deeply. "I love you too." His voice was shaky.

Harry kissed him again. "Show me."

Kit, red-faced, laid Harry back down and reached between them. He stroked his and Harry's cocks together, gathering the combined moisture spilling from them both. At the first touch of those hot, wet fingers to the sensitive skin around his entrance, Harry grunted and rolled his hips, struggling to keep still.

Kit kissed him and he stilled, allowing the pressure to build until Kit's fingers breached his body. He grunted again, recalling the hot pain just before the pleasure took over. He breathed and relaxed his muscles, watching Kit's brows furrow adorably in concertation. He didn't want to hurt Harry. He gently coaxed at Harry's pleasure until Harry grabbed Kit by the neck and snarled against his lips, "Stop teasing me."

"I don't want to hurt you."

"You won't. I'm ready, more than."

Kit finally gave a small chuckle. "Acting all brave and tough."

Harry smiled back. "About time."

Kit reared up. Harry opened his legs wider, ignoring the aches and pains of his beaten body. The powders took the edge off, his determination handled the rest. He pointed to the table. "The bottle on the right, it's oil."

Kit arched an eyebrow at him. "You're very prepared, Dr. Woodsman."

"It's for burns."

Kit dropped his brow and went to retrieve the bottle. He re-seated himself between Harry's legs, opening the bottle and giving it a curious sniff. He laced his fingers with Harry's scarred ones and brought Harry's wrist to his lips, breathing in. "I recognize the scent."

"You should. I used it on your brand."

Releasing Harry's hand, Kit unstoppered the bottle and drenched his fingers. He pressed his fingers once more inside Harry before slicking his length. Harry's chest heaved, the anticipation rising until he could barely stand it. He rubbed Kit's thighs, kneading the muscles. "Come on, love. I can't wait anymore."

"Me neither." Kit pushed forward.

He entered, the blunt head spreading Harry almost impossibly wide. Kit shuddered, gasping until he slid all the way in. He breathed out. "Harry."

"That's it," Harry panted. "Come here."

Kit fell atop him, trembling in Harry's arms. Stroking Kit's hair, getting his fingers tangled the sweaty clumps, Harry tugged him into a kiss. It was messy and breathless and was enough to start Kit grinding his hips. Tentatively at first, as the movement had Harry's muscles clenching instinctively. Harry hissed, but didn't let him stop, didn't want this feeling to stop. He clung to Kit, rolling his hips. Kit needed little encouragement, thrusting shallowly until Harry was groaning from deep in his throat, sucking and biting lightly at Kit's skin between breaths.

They fell into their own rhythm, desperately clinging to each other, slick skin sliding together, hot breath mingling. Kit gasped and slowed to a halt, reaching between them and grasping the base of his cock. Catching his breath, Harry said, "What's wrong?"

Kit's cheeks colored. "I'm close. I don't want this to end."

Harry smiled and stroked Kit's jawline and cheek. Kit nuzzled against the touch, the smallest glimmer of a tear wetting Harry's thumb. He wasn't sure if Kit was referring to sex or their time together. Either way the answer was the same. "It won't. I won't let it. We have time. Forever, if you want."

Kit swallowed hard.

"Please, Kit, don't stop. I want to see you when you release inside me. I want your heat. I want to remember this, the first time you made love to me."

Kit's cock flexed inside Harry, making him moan, which turned into a growl as Kit slid back inside, tight sac slapping Harry's skin, delicious pressure stroking Harry's prostate, his legs tensing before turning into mush with every unceasing swipe over that sensitive clutch of nerves. He gasped airlessly, grunted and called Kit's name as Kit's thrusts grew more persistent, more possessive until Harry's balls tightened and he clenched down on the heat invading his body. His orgasm hit, releasing a cascade of pleasure pulsing out of his body. His seed erupted from his cock, so powerful it arced up and hit Kit's stomach and chest, leaving Harry a quivering mess as Kit continued to grind against his prostate. Kit was not far behind, fucking liquid heat deep inside Harry, wringing out the last of his seed until they were both left breathless and boneless, Kit's face a picture of angelic bliss.

Kit collapsed atop Harry, fitting perfectly along his body, heedless of the sweat and seed mingling between them. Aches started to protest throughout Harry's body but he didn't care. He couldn't have moved Kit if he'd tried, nor did he want to. He lazily stroked the length of Kit's spine, pressing his nose against the damp curls clinging to his throat, feeling Kit's cock slowly soften and slip free of his body. It was more than he'd ever thought he deserved, and he held Kit until they both fell into a heavy doze.

* * * *

A moment of sheer panic struck Kit when he woke in Harry's bed. Alone. The bottles and their clothes had been tidied away. Kit was clean, dressed in a nightshirt and delightfully spent. He allowed his heart rate to normalize before rising, realizing what had woken him. Voices were coming from downstairs.

Pulling on his, no, Harry's loose trousers, he descended the first few steps before ducking down to take a look. The house was packed with people. Well, it looked packed when compared to how empty it usually was. There was a large table in the center. It was not one of Harry's creations — it must have been brought from the village. The crowd of people sitting or standing around it consisted of Amy and Davy, each with a red-faced, squealing infant in their arms. Next to them stood Thom, who was clapping Davy hard on the back and laughing at something he'd said. There was also the fishmonger and his father. Cole, Kit remembered. One of the men he would be eternally grateful to. There were other faces he recognized but could not put a name to, and they all spoke and joked amicably.

Harry was also sitting at the table in his usual chair, still looking bruised and battered, but smiling and a little flushed as food was pushed in front of him. He sat next to the old man, Francis, who was looking as beaten up as Harry, and next to him was his daughter Celeste along with some younger boys who had to be her brothers. Harry ate a little then, as though sensing Kit's presence, stopped and looked to the stairs.

Kit fought the ridiculous urge to hide and leave Harry to his friends, but instead stood and walked down to join them. More eyes turned to him, along with welcoming smiles. He met Celeste's eyes and shame heated his face at how he had acted the first time they'd met. He expected animosity, but was surprised when she said to him, "Are you hungry? We've got a little bit of everything. Help yourself."

Kit cleared his throat before saying, "Thank you."

He was starving, but he only picked at his food, some flatbread and roasted pork with applesauce. He caught Harry's gaze every now and then across the table, his eyes seeming to say, *'Are you all right?'* Kit offered a small smile in return.

Later a knock came at the door and more people poured in, going straight to Harry and asking after him, offering embraces and more food for the table. Over the last week or so while Harry had remained unconscious, Kit had had to deal with the relentless changing flow of people coming to see Harry and offer support. At the time the constant intrusions had itched as his patience, but he'd tolerated them, his only concern Harry's welfare. Now that Harry was up and greeting them himself, Kit had a gnawing sense he was now superfluous.

When the house became too hot and crowded with visitors, Kit slipped outside and paced absently around the yard until he came to the log he'd sat on with Harry weeks ago. He stared back at the house, listening to the rambling and laughter coming from within.

He was happy for Harry. He had so many people who loved and cared for him, whom he cared for in return. It was hard to see where Kit could fit in with them all, hard to not feel like a stranger intruding on their lives.

Harry loved him, had said as much, had shown him in many ways, yet something deeply embedded still wouldn't allow him to trust it. He knew what it was and it sickened him. Tariq, even as a ghost, dogged Kit's shadow, pushing his mistrust closer to the surface. How long would it take for Harry to grow weary of him, his possessiveness, his overbearing desire for constant affection and assurance? His chest grew tight. He didn't know if he could handle being thrown away again.

"Kit, what are you doing out here?"

Harry was making his way over, a little stiff, blinking as he stepped into the pool of sunlight filling the yard. Kit stood and went to him instead of watching him struggle all the way over. Harry took his hand, his smile tight and his pain obvious.

"I just needed some air."

"It is a bit much in there. I never imagined the house would one day be filled with so many people."

"You should go back in."

Harry eyed him with that same clinical stare he'd used when looking over Kit's wounds, assessing the damage, seeing how he could fix it. "Now I'm up and about they won't stay long. They'll go back to the village once they've ensured I've eaten as least three days' worth of food."

"You could go with them."

"They're fine. Francis let me have a look at his injuries and Amy and the twins are doing great."

"No, I mean...you could live in the village. You don't need to live out here on your own anymore."

"I won't be. I have you. Don't I?"

Kit swallowed at the crack in Harry's voice.

"You've changed your mind. You want to leave."

"No. I don't want to, but—"

"Then why? I don't understand."

Harry's hurt and frustration hit Kit like physical blows, the air leaving his lungs. He cleared his throat. "I don't...I don't want to become a burden to you. You have so many people who already rely on you. I don't want you to decide now and then regret choosing me further down the line. You could have a normal life, a real chance at happiness. I'll only serve as a reminder to all you suffered. I can't... I don't know how to make you happy."

Harry's brow was furrowed, his eyes dark. He knew, he already knew Kit was right. Kit closed his eyes, unable to watch Harry reach the same conclusion and agree to let Kit go. He jolted when Harry brushed his knuckles over his cheek. "Kit, you already do. This is the happiest I can recall being in a very long time. Will you allow me the chance to return the favor?"

Kit swallowed and blinked rapidly. Harry pulled on their laced hands, dragging Kit closer and dragging him into a tight embrace. He'd never had the chance to love someone normally after what Tariq turned him into, hadn't thought it was possible. But he'd never thought he'd meet someone like Harry, someone who had seen into the pits of darkness and still managed to hold onto the light.

"Kit, answer me, please."

Kit buried his head in Harry's shoulder, biting his lip to stifle the sob threatening to embarrass him further. His heart swelled in his chest, a sweet ache he couldn't recall feeling before. He sighed, clinging to Harry's shirtsleeve, summoning his courage to say, "You better not regret this, Dr. Woodsman."

Harry gave a choked laugh and pulled back to press a firm to kiss to Kit's mouth. Kit accepted it, deepening the kiss, ignoring the tears wetting his cheeks. Breaking the kiss, Harry pressed his forehead to Kit's. "Never."

Want to see more like this?
Here's a taster for you to enjoy!

Wolf of the West
Belinda Burke

Excerpt

Marcas stared upward at the sound of an imperative caw, and knew he must move faster. Four legs paced under him, swift as the wind, but he could see even from a distance that what had been a battlefield had now become a scavenger's rout. Above him, black crows crossed the sky, first in twos and threes, then a streaming murder.

It is coming.

The twilight darkened into premature night under the shadow of their wings, and from the gore that littered the field came crawling shadows, stick-figures unbending against the light.

Darkness made flesh.

Once, twice, Marcas howled, but the moon was not yet risen and he could summon no light into his service. From the top of a low rise, he could only look down and watch more carnage in the making. Warriors, bloodstained, wounded — waylaid in victory or defeat, they had survived the battle only to suffer something more terrible.

His gaze focused on their widened eyes, the glaring darkness in each overburdened pupil, teeth visible behind lips thinned with fear in each face — yet in none of them did he see what he had come for. A spark of light — *the mark of brightness* that told him the one so marked was meant to survive. That one, he would protect. But where was he?

Wraiths absent of flesh unfolded across the carnage, seeking their prey. The survivors who could move stumbled away from them with all the speed their broken limbs could muster. Marcas' gaze caught on three that moved together, two older, one younger, perhaps a son or nephew of one of the others. The elder two held him back, their hands across his chest at what they must have believed was a final moment of fear — and yet that youth stood forward, his face all confrontation, nothing of terror in the glare of his eyes.

The shadow moved to confront him, the youth painted with blazing light in the dark field of Marcas' mind, and the truth flamed in him, sudden and precise.

This one! This one — now, now!

In a flash, Marcas leaped down the hillside, crossed the blooded grass and buried his teeth in the shadow nearest the youth. Black blood spurted around his fangs, and he felt dark fingers clutching at the fur of his back. Marcas whipped around and lunged at them. He caught sight of the three men behind him, their eyes wider now, if that was possible — watching him, wondering — but there was no way for him to explain.

Like many men before them, they would have to come to their own conclusions.

Growling, spitting, pacing back and forth, Marcas marked a circle with his steps, with his body, with his flashing fangs. He leaped across to threaten any reaching hand, any open mouth, rattle-breathed, foaming.

Three of them, but I can't protect just that one. The boy. The boy wouldn't let me, and it wouldn't be right.

But three men were two more than he had expected. A battle like this one, wounds like theirs—the older men should probably be dead, but there was no accounting for the strength of a heart, a spirit or a warrior. Marcas' quick eyes took in the wound on the younger one—the thigh, wrapped tight, blood soaked but older blood now, not fresh flowing... *Not so bad, boy.* It would be easier to protect him than the other two—closer to death, closer to the enemy.

The crawling multitude of bloodthirsty spirits reached out first for the men, not the boy. For a moment he felt a vain desire to take the boy and leave these fools to their fate. One wounded young man was no match for a wolf of the *faoladh,* no matter what his desires.

But across his mind's eye flashed that first glimpse again—blazing light and eyes with no terror in them at all.

Black energies tore at his back again, gripped his tail and pulled him. He whirled, ears laid back, snapping, tasted darkness and congealed death, but it was neither blood nor anything real. Shadow screeched, a sound like the caw of the crows, but deepened, twisted, broken. He sought the matte jet throats, tore open wounds that spilled nothing, but it was nothing with the taste of ash. Marcas pushed them back with the weight of his body, with his claws and fangs that snapped with supernatural swiftness. Tireless, intent, he fought against the circling foes that increased in number even as he engaged them. They flowed back and receded, then returned to wash around him, a new and stronger tide—

Until the moon rose. The moonlight fell on Marcas' back and his fur shone with a pale light, every hair illuminated. He lifted his head and those of his foes closest to him took a step back. His mouth opened, and out of his throat came an illuminated noise, more than a howl—the true song of the night, safety from all shadow in that one note, even as it was many.

The wolf song shattered the shadow, broke it apart into bits as the moonlight spread and painted the black of the hills and the gore of the field with light. Panting now, feeling the pain of many wounds, Marcas fell silent and stepped back, looked around with wary eyes to see if the night might choose to rebirth its horrors.

There was only silence and stillness. The natural shadows of the night, death in coherent slumber. What the violence had awakened was restful now. *Quiet.*

Satisfied, Marcas turned to face the trio of men he had protected. They, too, were silent, all but unmoving, until he turned to leave.

"Wait."

It was a young voice, the voice of the one he'd been called to protect, but Marcas didn't look back. He turned away despite that call, and vanished into the cloak of the night.

* * * *

The dawn came early, yellow and heavy, sunlight spreading like spilled yolk across the horizon. It was welcome light, which scattered shadow and imprisoned the fears of the night behind walls of memory. The shapes of dark and crooked power that had spilled from what had once been the bodies of friends and foe—the tide of dark within the night—those things were faded, but the memory of that which had conquered them was not.

The wolf.

"Still well, Connor?"

Startled from the thoughts that had distracted him, the throbbing of the wound in Connor's thigh returned full force at the sound of his father's voice. He almost brought up the image that lingered in his mind's eye. *Moonstruck wolf.* But he hesitated, and only answered the question his father had asked.

"Well enough. I'll make it."

They lapsed into silence after that. As Connor limped forward beside the single horse they'd found wandering at the edge of the battlefield, he drew himself out of his thoughts and watched his father over the horse's neck. Silent, craggy, a mountain in motion, he stomped forward as if nothing could — or would — stop him, as if he felt neither the pain of his wounds nor the pain of their journey. How far now? Since the wolf had left them in the blazing moonlight — since they'd found the horse and his father had forced Lord Aran to mount? *Too long.*

There had been an apology on his father's face, as he'd shoved Aran up on the beast, but despite the agony of this stumble through the dark, there'd been no other way to keep Aran moving.

Again, Connor looked into his father's face. His dark eyes were crowded under the clenching of his brow and the poor bandage that was bound there. His father nodded once, approval or encouragement, and Connor set his eyes on the road again, a dusty band that cinched the green hills before them like a poorly tightened belt.

It was good that he hadn't said anything, hadn't brought up the questions that burned in him. When he had asked in the dark after the wolf had left them, his father had shushed him right away, warned of bad luck and spurned blessings. *Some things we should not speak of, even amongst ourselves.* He heard the echo of his father's voice, the only answer he'd gotten, and knew that now wasn't a time to add to his worries—but despite his outer silence, the questions remained inside him, loud and urgent.

What had those things been? Shadow had risen from their comrades and from the enemy warriors both. Was it the power of their foe? *But then, what of the wolf?* Where had he come from? He had never seen anyone fight the way that wolf fought. Focusing on those moments, those memories, he shuddered, stumbled, caught himself and forced himself not to look at his father again. *Some things weren't meant to be faced by mortal men.* He had seen training injuries enough and the wounds on returning warriors—he'd thought he'd known what there was to know of battle and death.

He knew better now.

Battle was not wounds and weapons and warriors. Battle was blood-smoke, a mist of red in the air, so fine the taste of it was in every breath. Battle was stepping forward and slipping and not looking down to see if what was under your boots was mud or the blood-slick guts of someone who didn't know he was dead yet. Connor had learned that the arm could grow so tired it couldn't stop swinging, that a blade new-sharpened could clot in a glut of flesh, chip on a sternum and still shatter a skull. Battle was heaving breath, every muscle burning and nerves dead ended or on fire—no in-between, no pause, no breathing space... And in the lulls, everything too quiet. Every crow's cawing, every breath of wind became a thing that stirred alertness out of impossible fatigue.

He'd thought the end was just another one of those lulls. That there would be another charge, another rush—something else, because it couldn't be over. It would never be over... But it was.

Until night came.

His leg had been long-bound by then and he had done what he could for his father, limping, reaching across the broad shoulders to bind a wound that streamed new flow over the rusty stains of old blood. But it had been Aran who was the worst wounded, by the loss of his sons. Connor had found him, bent over the bodies. Perhaps it had been Aran's cries that had woken shadows out of the dead. *They were loud enough. They went on forever.*

Not that he could blame him. There would be no honored burial, no pyre for those boys, not after this battle. Not when no one survived, no one but them — who would carry the bodies? Who would return to this plain and bring away the crow's feast that remained? They had come to the very edge of his father's kingdom to fight, two hundred warriors seeking to spill blood in the name of an ancient feud long abated. Fifty years of the High King's peace had been broken there, and for what?

Nothing had been won, nothing gained, nothing threatened — a field in the middle of pastureland, and no herds in sight, and now his father's men and the men who had rebelled both were dead.

Connor sighed, licked dry lips and looked up across the endless rolling of the hills and into the sunlight. *How much farther?* He took another step, and another, and another…

"Connor? Stop, Connor."

He heard his father's voice, but it seemed to come from a distance. Why would that be? His father was…right there. He turned his head to the left, and the motion unbalanced some precarious state he hadn't even been aware of. His head was light, and his leg was numb. Thigh to foot, he couldn't feel a thing.

"That isn't right…"

"Connor!"

Darkness.

It reached out to envelop him, and for an instant, his heart sped up in fear.

But no.

No worries.

The thought came to him of itself, soothing, silken.

Wolf will protect me.

There was no need to fear the night.

Sign up for our newsletter and find out about all our romance book releases, eBook sales and promotions, sneak peeks and FREE romance books!

About the Author

Born and bred in the Midlands, Lucien spends most of his time inside his small bedroom/library/office reading and writing gay fiction, sacrificing his wardrobe space for his bookcases.

Stumbling upon Yaoi in his teens, Lucien's passion for gay romance/erotica began, starting his once small, now consuming book collection. Not too long after, he started writing his own fiction and never looked back, even writing a lesbian themed short story in his GSCE English exam.

While a fan of most subgenres, he enjoys writing historical, fantasy and BDSM stories.

Lucien loves to hear from readers. You can find his contact information, website details and author profile page at https://www.pride-publishing.com